Samantha

Malania E. Reynolds

THREE SKILLET

Samantha

THREE SKILLET

www.ThreeSkilletPublishing.com

Cover typesetting and formatting by Farley Dunn

This is a work of fiction based on actual historical places and events. The author has referenced certain historical figures for context and realism, but all characters are fictitious, and any resemblance to actual persons living or dead, except in a general historical context, is purely coincidental.

ISBN: 978-1-943189-34-2

— 1 —

Major Jeremiah Delaney Watson dominated the family portrait hanging proudly over the elaborate marble fireplace in the parlor of his Alexandria, Virginia, home. A giant of a man, both in physical stature and in reputation, he was a hero in the late war, and currently a lawyer and merchant by trade; and quite wealthy by current society standards. His portrait reflected his position in society, with its carved, gold filigree frame and matching sconces hanging on either side, surrounded by swaths of hand-painted silk wall coverings. Custom-designed, the sconces sported leaded glass globes and shimmering oil reservoirs; and they glittered with bright spots of flame, imbuing a shadowy life into the images surrounding the major.

His daughters Charlotte and Marguerite stood on his left, dressed in teal and burgundy, with ermine stoles across their shoulders, and their hair wound into fanciful designs. A stuffed bird nestled in Charlotte's hair, while Marguerite touted a feathered hat, tilted jauntily on one side. Directly behind her, with only his head and shoulders visible between the girls, appeared his son, Thomas, his dark hair overly long and his face almost hidden in the shadows.

Frederick, aged twelve, stood next to his mother, Martha, and wore a mischievous grin on his round face. Martha, her face stern and her frock a flattering shade of lavender, was seated on an overstuffed brocade chair, holding baby Sally dressed in a white dedication gown, embroidered with open cutwork and studded with freshwater pearls. Ten-year-old Arthur seemed as if he would burst from the image, come alive in oil and flesh, if not held on the shoulder by the most striking person in the painting. Almost as if glowing, his sister Samantha, stunningly fresh and youthful at seventeen, smiled down from the wall as if ready to welcome visitors into the family home. Her gown was of pink silk organdy, with puffed sleeves, and it shimmered as if alive. Her hair, piled high on her head, caught the light, and the ribbons woven into her tresses set off her gentle blue eyes.

One place was empty in the portrait; Matthew, the eldest at twenty-four, was in Florida when the portrait was commissioned. He was unable to excuse himself from his duties as 2nd lieutenant in the Army to return home at the time of the sitting.

On this frosty day in January, while the rest of the family was occupied elsewhere, Major Watson enjoyed a stiff of brandy, with an open decanter at his side. A fire crackled in the fireplace, cheerily warming the massive room. He gazed at the portrait and was pleased that he'd chosen the right artist to capture the likeness of his prodigy. He focused on the face of his dear wife and flinched when Abigail, the family's faithful housekeeper, rang a small bell and paused just outside the room.

"Yes, Abigail?" Major Watson held his glass high in greeting, calling to her. "How may I help you today?"

"A letter, sir, by special courier." She nodded and bobbed in a half-inflected curtsey.

"Let me have it, then." He set his glass down and held out his hand.

"I cannot, sir. I'm afraid it's only for your hand." She moved aside to reveal the red-and-gold livery of a footman who stepped forward and nodded his head respectfully.

"Come forward, man," Watson called, standing.

"Major Watson, sir. I was told by Colonel Livingston to hand this directly to you." The footman pulled a folded paper sealed with wax from his coat pocket and held it out to the major. The man's hat was pulled hard against his ears, and he shivered in the warmth of the room.

"From Colonel Livingston?"

"Aye, sir. From the colonel's own hand. He said I was to give it to you only."

Watson took the missive and instructed Abigail to give the man something for his efforts. The door was closed quietly behind the servants, and he paused a moment to reflect on the surprise intrusion into his day. Seating himself and adjusting his position to soak as much warmth as possible from the fire, he snapped the wax seal with a thin knife and began to read.

Wash. Cty, 4 Jan. '92

To my Good Friend, Maj. Watson, Greetings:

As I am confident the Maj. remembers from our last Meeting, I am in poss. of a Military Warrant for a large Acreage in W. Virginia in the area now called Kentucky for my Services in the War. I must soon take Action on the Property or risk losing my Right to Occupy the parcel. I am writing to beg you, as my Friend, to help me make this Claim upon my Warrant.

Among my Relations in Baltimore is a merchant named F. Prescott. After some debate with P. about the Settlement of the Acreage, it has been decided that his Neph, Andrew Prescott, is quite able to take on the Responsibility of clearing the land and organizing a Settlement for pioneers willing to tackle the wild Animals and native Peoples of the area. I cannot take on the Position myself because of my Advanced Age and current Ill health. I have spoken with A. Prescott and am assured that he is Experienced and Skilled in the administration of a large Plantation and has a vast Knowledge of Survival in the Wilderness. He has successfully completed two Trips to the Mountains of W. Virginia and into the Wilds of Pennsylvania, and has lived for some time in K.

For A.P. to be successful in the endeavor, young Prescott requires the assistance of a wife, able to cope with the Hardship and Danger of an Adventurous Life. While pondering the Matter, it was brought to my mind that my Friend, Maj. W, already living in Virginia, has a Daughter of Marriageable age. Would my Friend agree that a Match between A. Prescott and S. Watson be Feasible and Profitable to us both? As Wife of the younger Prescott, S. would naturally be given a Portion of the Land as her dower right. Please answer soon as the Matter should be settled before the early Spring thaws. Young P. is anxious to start on his Task in time for the early plowing Season.

I remain yr. obed. Ser. and Friend, Colonel O. Livingston.

Watson sat a moment, stunned by the missive and request of his old comrade-in-arms. He found his glass, finished the brandy inside and poured another inch in the glass from the decanter, and downed it in one gulp.

Without thought to his aching knees, Watson walked upstairs to share the news with his wife, sitting among the younger children in the classroom. They agreed after some discussion that the colonel needed a speedy reply to his proposal, and the major went more slowly and reflectively down the stairs to his study. He sat for some time in fond memories of his friendship with Livingston, and with a smile on his florid face, he began to make plans for his daughter's future.

He drew paper from his secretary, and sharpening his feather pen with a small knife he used for the purpose, dipped it into the India ink bottle and began to write. Satisfied with his task, he covered his body with his heavy coat, pulled a colorful wool scarf woven by his wife around his neck, and walked to the stables. It was a harsh, cold day, and the wind stung his cheeks. He called to the groom, gave him the letter and instructions and sent him on his way to Washington City. Later, sitting in his library with smoke circling his head from his lighted pipe, he thought how best to tell his daughter of his plan for her future.

— 2 —

Samantha and her sister Marguerite were sitting in hard back chairs in the back parlor, knitting socks for the younger children. There was a cozy fire burning in the fireplace, but still there was a chill near the windows of the room. Sammie glanced out the window where she could just see the limbs of a tall tree scraping mournfully against the window pane. Marguerite was chattering on about the new tutor hired to teach Frederick and Arthur the rudiments of Latin. Sammie, if she had her wish, would rather be in the classroom, listening to the tutor, but her mother disapproved of higher education for females, so the older girls had been banished from the school-room while the lessons commenced. Through the open door, she could hear her sister Charlotte in the music room practicing her scales on the pianoforte. She heard a scratching at the hallway door and called for the person to enter.

The footman, Jem, stood at the door, his eyes quickly darting around the room before settling on Sammie.

"Miss Watson, the major says you are to come to his office right away." The tuft of hair that always seemed to hang low on his forehead couldn't keep the curiosity from his eyes.

"Thank you, Jem. You may go."

"Yes, Miss Watson." He bowed low and backed politely out of the room, closing the door softly behind him.

"Oh, my, Sammie, what have you done?" Marguerite inquired.

Without answering, Sammie frowned as she collected her knitting and placed it in the box at her side. She couldn't think what was so important that she must leave her tasks behind. She noted the reflection of sympathy in Marguerite's eyes as she left the room and hurried down the hallway to answer her father's summons. The hall was chilled, and Sammie shivered and drew her shawl closer to her shoulders as she scratched on the door. It was early January, and despite the fireplaces and Ben Franklin stoves in the larger rooms, the hallway in the large white house wasn't heated.

"Come in," came Jeremiah Watson's gruff voice. She stepped lively through the door and walked to the desk in the corner. She gazed at the magnitude of books on the shelves and sighed. She never seemed to have enough time to read, and besides baking in the kitchen, it was almost her favorite pastime.

"You wanted to see me, Father?" Sammie had started calling her father by the formal name when she turned ten and was chastised for racing her pony through the streets of Alexandria without a groom in attendance. She'd been sent to bed without her supper as punishment and hadn't quite forgiven him for the indignity, since she had been accustomed to riding with her older brothers without restraint. Her mother had strongly disapproved of her behavior, and told her that she should always remember she was a lady, and her father a most important man in the city. She began to see her father in a new light. He was no longer the jolly man of games and playful demeanor, but a stern man of discipline and strict obedience. She hadn't forgotten the incident, and her deportment had changed into the quiet, reticent manner of today.

"Sit down, Daughter. I've something of grave importance to discuss with you." He came from behind the desk and stood for a moment at the window, gazing out at the tranquil scene without actually seeing it. His back was straight and his dark hair was curly and long, tied in an old-fashioned queue, and covering his ears.

Sammie sat with her hands folded in her lap. She took a sly glance toward the picture on the opposite wall, a vase with multicolored flowers on a table. She loved the colors and the graceful lines. She liked to sketch and paint. She spent as much time as available to her with her watercolors and charcoal pencils. She was a keen observer of nature, the birds and insects, and shapes and details of trees. But, most interesting were the flowers in her mother's small garden. She'd filled pages and pages of paper with watercolors of flowers, and placed them in a book, enclosed between two thin boards, and tied with a pink ribbon. She kept it hidden under her bed, for she didn't want her younger siblings to harm it. Suddenly, she straightened and brought a smile to her face, when her father sat beside her in a cushioned chair. She sobered when she saw the frown on his brow.

"Sammie, I'd thought to wait until you were older to bring

forth the matter of your marriage; when you had time to adjust to the thought of adult responsibilities and more experience with the traditions of modern society." He glanced toward the fireplace and sighed. His large hands fidgeted, and he coughed in embarrassment.

Samantha gulped. "Marriage, sir?" She hadn't thought of marriage for herself. Naturally, she knew that her father would arrange a match for her, as was the custom in their circle, but she thought it would be far in the future. Why, she had only this past summer been allowed to attend her parents' frequent tea parties and formal dinners.

"Yes. Marriage. It's a serious matter and one that I would have postponed, if I hadn't received a most beneficial request from my friend, Colonel Livingston, in Washington. Please listen to what I have to say before you interrupt." He looked troubled and moved to take her hands into his larger ones. She could feel the strength in his hands. She glanced into his eyes, and he withdrew and sat back in his chair. He cleared his throat.

"Father, I cannot be married." She interrupted, stammering her words, the realization sinking in. She was a girl, still, and she had no desire to become a wife for some time. He ignored her protest.

"Be silent. I've accepted the proposal of marriage on your behalf. You must be brave and accept this decision with grace and loyalty to your family. The deed is done, and if you don't cooperate, it will bring dishonor and disgrace to your mother, your brothers and sisters, and possibly take years to repair the damage to our reputation."

"I don't understand, Father. How would I bring dishonor to everyone? Isn't my duty to obey you and marry the man of your

14

choice? Mother said that I shouldn't set my cap at the young men of my acquaintance, for it's the accepted thing in our higher circle of society for the elder daughters to marry for the advantage of the family. I'll obey you in this matter, for I trust your judgment and respect your high standards." Sammie rung her hands and wished she had a handkerchief, for she felt humbled and slightly sick at her stomach.

"That's better." He watched her intently.

"Who is he, Father? What must I do to prepare for my future husband? Will you please explain? Won't we live as I do now, in the city of Alexandria?"

"No, my daughter. That's what I must explain. Please listen carefully, and don't interrupt." Major Watson stood and again walked to the window and looked out. Sammie watched him with trepidation and fear in her heart. She gazed up at the picture above the fireplace and a tear fell from her eye. Not live in Alexandria? Not attend the parties and balls, and paint the flowers in the garden? She jumped when the man suddenly turned and came back to her. He loomed over her for a moment, and she quaked in his presence. He paced the room, then seemed to make a decision, and sat down in the chair beside her. This time he took her hands in his, and she trembled.

"Daughter, when you were a very small girl, Colonel Livingston and I and many other men of our generation went off to war. It was a different world then; for the country about us still belonged to Great Britain. Maryland, Virginia and Pennsylvania were not yet a part of the United States of America. In fact, we weren't a country until Thomas Jefferson of Virginia wrote the Declaration of Independence, and the Congress gave authority to General Washington to wage war against the British. But, we persevered and won our independence from the tyranny of London. We are as you see us now, a cluster of states along the eastern seacoast. For our service in the war, we were given bounty warrants for land in the interior; that is, a place called Kentucky. It's wild, uncultivated land and populated by the heathen red Indians and wild beasts. But, you mustn't be alarmed, for God will watch over you."

"Indians, Father? Oh, say it isn't so!"

He dropped her hands, rose and paced the room again. Sammie began to see a vision of the man she was to marry, and she sighed deeply. Her father had chosen one of his contemporaries, an old man with a bald head and no teeth, and a long gray beard. How would she stand it, being married to such a man? She would die. She knew she would.

He must have seen the look of fear in her eyes, for he came back and sat down. He took her hands and smoothed the skin of her palms. He began to speak.

"Colonel Livingston won in the lottery a large acreage in the wilderness. He's now infirm and he needs someone young and strong to clear the land for settlement and build a town, or he'll lose his warrant. He's chosen a man of ability named Andrew Prescott, who's to be your husband. I don't know the man, but I know his uncle by reputation. If the nephew is half as good a woodsman and marksman, he'll be able to care for you well. He needs a wife to support him in his endeavors, to cook his meals, wash and mend his clothing, and comfort him in the night. Your mother will instruct you in your duties. It'll be a hard life, and you'll be far from your family and friends, but you're a strong woman, and loyal. There will be other women in the settlement, so you won't be cut off from female companionship. I've written my permission for the match. We must wait for Colonel Livingston's reply. Maybe the plans are changed. In the meantime, you're to prepare yourself for a life in the wilderness. You must attend to your regular duties until your betrothed comes to fetch you." He dropped her hands and rose.

"But Father, didn't you receive a land warrant in Kentucky? I don't understand."

He looked at her and smiled. "Aye, Sammie, I was offered the land in payment for my services but knew quite well that your mother would never accept such a life away from her friends and family in the city, so I refused the offer, and I'm content with my choice, for you know I love the excitement and glamor of the political life as well as Martha. I'd almost forgotten that until I received the missive from my friend. Maybe Matthew or Thomas will try someday when they're older to apply for some land, if it isn't too late. It'll be their choice." He smiled as though visualizing his sons in the wilderness, and Sammie was no longer afraid.

"Now, buck up, Daughter. Don't be afraid; our loving God will help you in your new situation. Pray with me, now." Sammie bowed her head and listened to her father drone on in a sing-song voice, but her mind was far from worship. She was thinking that her husband was a young man, not a toothless wizard. Her heart beat with relief, and she almost skipped up the stairs. She was halfway before she realized that she'd been knitting in the back parlor and retraced her steps to join her sisters, who questioned her endlessly on her upcoming marriage.

Sammie lay that night in the darkness in the bed with her

sisters, Charlotte and Marguerite, thinking of Andrew Prescott, her betrothed. Would he be tall and dark? Or, short and light of complexion, and drink too much, like her brother Matthew? She'd heard her parents discuss her brother's vanity and faults when they didn't suspect she was nearby. He'd been gone from home for many months, and she could barely recall his face. She shuddered and pulled the covers more tightly around her shoulders.

Disturbed by her thoughts, she rose, lighted a candle and stood in front of the cheval mirror in the corner of the room. She removed her gown and leaned in to see her body in the glass. Her nose was too short, her mouth too full; and her eyes seemed dull with bushy brows. Her gaze went farther to the torso and hips; and down her long thin legs, past the black spot caused by the imperfection in the glass, which distorted the sight of her flat, narrow feet. She took a comb from the dressing table, parted her long hair and held it up into a knot on top of her head so she could see her neck. She turned a bit and leaned her head just so, in order to gaze at her back, and heard a sound from the bed. She let the hair fall around her shoulders and turned toward the bed.

It was her sister Marguerite. "What are you doing, Sammie? Aren't you coming to bed?"

Quickly, she grabbed her gown, pulled it over her head and let the cloth fall to her feet. She blew out the candle and climbed into the bed.

"Shush, don't tell Mama. I was only looking at myself. Go to sleep." She held her breath for a moment and relaxed when she heard her sister's soft snore. She sighed and turned toward the dying embers in the fireplace. A picture of her father's somber face drifted into her mind, and she knew her life would be different from this night on. The acceptance missive was even now making its way to Washington City; the guests would soon be snickering and laughing at her. How could any man desire such a simpleton with an imperfect body such as hers, she asked herself.

Charlotte murmured in her sleep and turned over. Sammie chuckled under her breath. Darling Charlotte and the other children. She would miss their loving caresses and odd ways. Suddenly, a tear gathered at the side of her nose; she would never see her brothers and sisters again, once she moved into the wilderness; she knew she wouldn't. She turned her face to the wall and wept.

January 6, 1792

It has Rained hard all day & I fear with the nightfall we will have snow. I can see from my chair the dead limbs on the oak tree outside my window. Father told me today of the plan he has made for my Future. It is to be a trek into the wilderness of the new country, Kantuckie. I shall have to Submit myself to his will. It is the Law of the land & who am I to say that one man is a better husband than another? His name is Andrew Prescott & he is from Baltimore. Can any good come from such a Place?

— 3 —

Sammie knew the day her father received the letter by special courier from Colonel Livingston, sealing her fate, for she understood the sudden bustle of activity and the significance of the visit from his friend and partner, the lawyer Mortimer Adar. They stayed holed up in his office for hours, it seemed, and Adar closed the office door softly behind him, carrying his thick leather satchel under an arm.

Adar brushed past Sammie, passing in the front hallway, and spoke with a sly grin on his face, "Aye, Miss Watson, 'tis a fine morning, indeed; the colonel will be pleased with this contract. I bid you adieu."

He patted the satchel, tipped his hat, and cackled with a mordant glee. She noticed the frayed cuffs at his wrists as he swept out the front door, his pale face shining in the glow from the sun, and his short queue tied with black ribbon. She stood for a moment, puzzled, then continued up the stairwell to the schoolroom.

January 14, 1792

To think that it has been a week since Father told me of the arrangements made on my behalf & we have heard no news of A. Prescott. We are in daily anticipation of his arrival to begin the courting period. Mama tells me it's my duty to be a good Wife unto him, but I fear I cannot. My spirit rebels at being away from the society parties and balls, for I love to dance. It hardly bears consideration as it depresses me very much. I attended the opera with Mama and Father last evening, and the male vocalist was vastly entertaining. He stumbled on a step, and Father remarked in the carriage that he must have been drinking, but Mama said we cannot judge. Charlotte had spent an hour with the curling iron, but my Hair does not conform to her high hopes of addressing the latest Style. Today, I helped Sally & Arthur with their schooling for we have lost another governess & Father has determined that Freddie is old enough to attend the local public school. The snow of a week ago has melted and I was able to walk in the garden, but alas there are no flowers to brighten the day.

— 4 —

The next few days flew past with an excitement and justifiable trepidation for the young Samantha. One hour she was helpful and looking forward to meeting Andrew Prescott; the next hour, she was sulking and resentful that she should have to leave behind all this laughter and comfort and love of her family. She wanted, instead, the lawn parties and the coquettish teasing with boys that she'd barely learned to enjoy. Clothing was selected and rejected, packed and unpacked, as her mother chose good, plain but durable materials and styles. It was doubtful that Sammie would need the silks and velvet frocks of her town social activities; she needed thick stockings, high-topped boots, heavy winter coats, and leather or wool gloves; and bonnets and broad-brimmed hats to protect her delicate skin from frostbite, blaring sun and insect bites.

Her precious tea pot and four cups were wrapped securely to prevent breakage and tucked in a small metal box in the corner of her trunk. A wooden crate held a china service for four, packed securely in sawdust. Another box hidden among the straw contained sewing notions such as thread, needles, pins, buttons, lace and knitting yarn. In another larger, metal water-proofed box was a supply of artist's material, for Sammie declared with a loud voice of protest that she would not leave the house without her greatest possessions. Her father stormed out of the house and left the decision of what to take to her mother. Over and over he admonished them to keep the baggage simple, that less was better, for she would be traveling by wagon, boat and even horseback or on foot through the wilderness.

At last, word reached the house that Andrew Prescott was a few miles away from the town. He was accompanied by his uncle, Franklin Prescott, and aunt, Jemima Crocket, who wanted to meet the young bride's family and give their approval to the match. They spent the final night of their journey in an inn about five miles away from Alexandria, and arrived at the Watson home about midmorning of the next day, a Thursday. Charlotte and Marguerite leaned far out the upstairs window as they heard the sound of horses' hooves. There was a long parade of horseback riders, carriages and mule-driven wagons; and the girls squealed with excitement and withdrew their heads to clamber down the stairs and run into the room with a swirl of skirts to meet the disapproval of their parents. They sat meekly on the sofa near the fireplace, hardly able to contain their tumult of joy. Charlotte pinched herself to make sure it was real.

Samantha sat in the corner in a stuffed silk-covered chair with a somber look on her countenance. Her heart was aflutter, and her breath came in pants. She took a few deep breaths and tried to calm herself as the knocker on the door was struck. She rose politely when the room filled with strangers, and she curtsied as each one was introduced to her; but her eyes searched for the one person who meant more than any society matron or gentlemen. He was not there.

Jemima Crocket was a stout, loud-voiced matron of undetermined age, dressed in darkest purple, who immediately took offense at the arrangements that had been made for the wedding. Looking over her horn-rimmed glasses at the bride, she gave her a look of disdain that sent Samantha into a quake of panic; but she held her head high and her face calm of expression.

"I do not approve of this haste into a marriage of convenience between strangers, Mrs. Watson, but am persuaded by the colonel that it's necessary if my nephew is to live in the wilderness of Kentucky. She's still a girl. This I hadn't expected." Jemima drew herself up and waved her finger in front of Martha's nose like a commander of troops, as if to make Samantha mature at her command. Yet she glanced at Sammie in a moment of discerning evaluation, seeming not at all displeased, as if the revelation of the girl's youth might be a boon she hadn't considered.

Sammie thought the woman looked like a bantam rooster giving orders to a peacock, for all the difference in sexes. She kept her face set and her eyes focused on the floor as she was discussed, as though she weren't in the room to hear the qualms about her character.

Martha smiled and kept her own feelings at bay. She lifted the china tea pot and poured the steaming liquid into cups, which Charlotte had been relegated to pass around to the throng. She motioned for the Watson footman to pass among the guests with a tray of tiny sandwiches and iced cakes. When she had finished, Charlotte sat and whispered to Marguerite, who responded with a smirk. Their mother gave the girls a stern look, and they subsided while they drank their tea.

Sammie took her cup, sipped slowly and remembered what she'd been told about appearances in public. She must remain cognizant of the fact that Jemima was a guest in their house. The younger girls listened and watched, fascinated by the gregarious woman and her dominant, outrageous mannerisms and actions.

Franklin Prescott was a short, stubby man of somber manner. He wore a coat of deepest blue, with a silver waistcoat and cream pants, with gold-tinted buckled shoes. He shook hands with the major, bowed to the ladies and broke into the conversation long enough to inform the host that his nephew was attending to the welfare of the animals and making arrangements for the storage of the luggage and supplies until after the wedding. The information was ignored by his sister-in-law, and she continued to prattle on with her opinion of hastily concocted marriage plans and launched into a lengthy lecture on traveling into the frontier without a troop of soldiers to protect them from danger. Prescott took a chair and watched lazily as his sister-in-law took over the situation.

Jemima's maid was given no chance to speak, but was pointed to a seat against the wall. Sammie glanced at her briefly and could see that she was very slender, had dark hair and a beak nose; her eyes appeared small and puffy, and she had a handkerchief in her hand, as though she'd been weeping. She wore a black wool cape, and one brown shoe peeped from under a dark gray skirt. She sipped her tea daintily, with her little finger held high and apart from the handle of the cup. She took more than her share of the thin ham sandwiches, and bit into them like she hadn't eaten a meal in months, her white teeth straight and like pearls on a string. She barely swallowed before Jemima Crockett spoke again.

Samantha's sisters could hardly pay attention to their own sewing, even though it was putting simple hems on white kerchiefs, as all their attention was devoted to Andrew's aunt and her boisterous way of commandeering any conversation around her. The whispers fluttered between the two girls, becoming more and more careless.

"Hush, sisters. The woman will hear you." Sammie did her best, to no avail.

"But, she's such a fascination. How could any woman be so rude?" Charlotte tittered, putting her hand to her mouth to try to contain it.

"We're beguiled by all her finery and her extreme beauty." Marguerite flipped her hair to the side and doubled over in barely-contained laughter.

"Mrs. Watson, you may need to correct your daughters. They seem to be unaware that this is a serious gathering, not a society fete for laughter and disruption." Jemima Crocket stiffened her spine, sniffing and looking down her nose at the two whispering females.

"Girls, Mrs. Crocket is correct. Tame your tongues." Their mother shushed them, but she wore a smile of her own as she did so, even if she took the time to remove it before returning her attention to the older woman.

"Now, Mrs. Watson, I've always believed that the bride should wear a veil. It adds a mystery to the occasion. I shall take

Samantha tomorrow in my own carriage to the shops and see that she has a proper veil." She peered at Sammie through the spectacles on her nose. "I see that her eyes are a true blue. That is to her advantage, of course, but the brows; they must be plucked. I'll see that my maid is available to her. She is experienced in the proper grooming of a lady." She took another sandwich and began to munch on it. No one dared move or speak. "And, the flowers, I cannot think that money should be spent on fresh flowers that last for only one hour. It's too frivolous. I shall cancel the order with the florist." She finished her sandwich and took a sip of tea.

"No, you cannot! I will not allow you to cancel the order. They are essential to the service." At last, Martha Watson found her courage and rose to her feet in protest, aghast that the woman would countermand her authority in the matter. And, to the astonishment of her daughters, she stamped her foot, stirring even her husband to life.

"Prescott, if you please; Thomas, my boy, I believe it's time for the males to retreat from the battlefield. I believe we have an offer of refreshments more to our tastes in the other room. Do not dawdle." Major Watson clapped his son Thomas on the shoulder and left the room, with the young man and Prescott following meekly behind to enjoy the quiet and comfort of his office, beyond the sound of shrill women's voices.

At last, when Sammie was ready to scream and run from the room in shame and horror, Martha rose from her seat and suggested that her guest might like to tidy herself after such a grueling day of travel. They left the room, and Sammie sighed in relief. She hardly heard the discussion of her sisters as she tried to guess what there was about her that the woman didn't like. Her fingers itched to move her charcoals across a sheet of paper to draw the features of her new relation while the impression of this first visit was fresh on her mind. So concentrated on the vision was she, that she didn't notice when her sisters left the room, clucking like hens in the barnyard.

Sammie raised her eyes with dismay when she heard the cough of a strange man standing near the doorway. He was very tall, with a ruddy complexion, and dressed in the latest style of long pants and wool waistcoat, with his hair cut short and his hands hanging limply at his side. She gasped and jumped to her feet. "Oh." It was all she could muster in her surprise at his appearance.

"Hello. I'm Andrew Prescott. I hope I have the honor of addressing Miss Samantha Watson?"

It was said with such charm that Sammie laughed and covered her mouth with consternation to be caught in such an uncouth manner.

"Please, don't be alarmed. I'd supposed that the family was still in attendance. Should I remove myself and come back later?" His eyes twinkled in merriment, and she relaxed. She took a few steps forward.

"Yes, I'm Samantha. How do you do, Mr. Prescott?"

"I must admit, I'd expected someone, umm," and he began to flush underneath his collar, "less youthful. I'm most surprised. Don't take me wrong, as I mean no offense. You're quite mature, just, um . . ." His voice died away, and he pulled at his collar with one hand.

She bristled, "I'm a woman, in every important way." Sammie was appalled that he expected someone more mature. She remembered her mother's words, that she must always present herself as happy and pleased; and she firmed her resolve that he would never know her doubts of herself.

"I'm pleased to hear it." He gave a small bow with a sarcastic smile. "I haven't offended you?"

"Of course not. You'll find that you're very welcome in this house. Have you finished your provisions for the animals and supplies? Your uncle told us that was the reason for the delay in your appearance." She gave him her hand, and he bowed and kissed the knuckles of each finger and turned it over and kissed her palm. Sammie blushed with surprise. When he looked up, she saw a light in his eyes she hadn't seen from a man before and puzzled over its meaning. She felt warmth spread over her. Her heart rate quickened, and she wished she hadn't eaten the sandwiches.

"Well, then, Miss Watson, shall we start afresh? It's a pleasure to meet you. Yes, I've made the animals comfortable for the night and found a small storage room at a local inn which will serve for the purpose until we leave on our journey into the unknown." There was a question in his eyes, and he stood stiffly in front of her, having dropped her hand politely.

Samantha smiled happily. She couldn't help it. She liked this man. She would be proud to be his partner and companion.

"I suppose I shouldn't speak of our approaching marriage without being first properly introduced, but you'll find that I'm shamelessly outspoken and direct. I'm delighted to see that you're handsome and young, for when my father first approached me with his plans for my future, I pictured you as an old man, toothless and bald. I'm very happy to see you are neither. Now, forgive me, I must remove myself from your presence before someone comes in. There are some sandwiches left if you're hungry, but I fear the tea is cold and unpalatable." She smiled again and swiftly left the room before he could answer.

She walked sedately up the stairs and into the room she would share with her sisters for only a few more nights. They were chattering excitedly. Charlotte was brushing her hair, and Marguerite was attempting to remove her dress but couldn't reach the tiny buttons at her back. Sammie moved to help her, her face still warm from her interaction with Andrew. She felt aglow with excitement. Her sisters continued talking as she moved to her desk, took out her charcoals and a sheet of clean paper and began to sketch the face and head of her nemesis, Jemima Crockett.

She remained happily engaged in her task and wasn't disturbed by her sisters' presence in the room. They left her undisturbed, as Sammie was always sketching or painting in their presence.

At last, as the shadows grew long in the room, she put her sketches and her charcoals away and began to dress for dinner. She looked at her wardrobe and withdrew the pale green silk gown which made her blue eyes change color and her dark brown hair soften the harsh prominence of her nose. She wasn't as lovely as her sisters, but she had a charming smile, clear skin and no freckles like those which already spotted the face of her sister Sally.

She wouldn't be able to wear this dress again. Her mother had already decided to leave her frills and fancy frocks behind for her sisters. It was a pretty picture as the three girls contended for space in front of the looking glass. The younger girls, Marguerite in yellow and Charlotte in pink, were still in the schoolroom, but their mother had said they might attend the festivities of the week, for they wouldn't have a chance to see their visitors for long. Their father had given his permission, and they swept down the stairwell in a flood of color and gay laughter. They stopped at the entrance to the parlor and made their entrance in a more sedate manner.

The room seemed filled with people, as indeed it was, and Sammie hesitated for an instant, before she followed her sisters into the room. Everyone turned and gazed at her, each with his or her own expression of curiosity and wonder at the beauty she displayed in her green gown, her hair curled in soft brown ringlets about her neck. She'd taken great care with her hair, hoping it wouldn't become tangled before the night had ended. Charlotte had helped her with the curling irons, for she enjoyed working with her sister's hair, pinning and twisting the strands into different styles. Sammie glanced around and smiled, shy but resolute.

"Daughter, how lovely and mature you look today. Have you had occasion to meet your betrothed?" Major Jeremiah Watson took his daughter's elbow and shifted her position to take in the dapper young man who had risen at her entrance. He spoke with confidence; revealing the pride he felt in his match-making skills.

Sammie caught Andrew's eye, and she fought a smile, certain her father would feel less assured if he knew of their previous meeting. It gave her a small thrill of anticipation, as if she were grown up, already an adventuress even though she'd yet to spend a day outside her father's home.

"Mr. Prescott, may I present to you my eldest daughter, Samantha Varella Watson. Sammie, my dear, here is your betrothed come to claim his right to your hand and heart in the holy rite of matrimony." Andrew bowed low over her hand, and she answered his gesture with a deep curtsey, rose and smiled.

The major turned to his interested audience, and in particular the dismayed Jemima Crockett, who was quickly revising her opinion of the match, for indeed the young woman was beautiful in her glamorous gown of pale green; and she seemed well mannered and shy.

"Come to me, Andrew." Jemima struck the floor with her cane. Obediently, he complied, and they sat conversing while the Major drew the attention of Franklin Prescott to the massive painting above the fireplace of his impressive family. Sammie heard him mention Matthew, far off with his Army unit. The talk became general in terms, and the affianced couple had no words with each other, as they were swept into the prevailing society gossip and talk of politics of the day. The latter, of course, was the special topic that engaged the bride's father at all times, and he soon had separated his son, Thomas; the elder Prescott; and his nephew, Andrew, from the ladies. Thomas grew quickly bored and was hard pressed to keep from yawning, but acted politely as he was required by his parents' high standards.

Sammie found herself commandeered by her mother and Jemima Crocket and tried her best to stay interested in their conversation, but found her mind wandering to the group of men by the fireplace. She was glad when the cook, Minerva Short, announced dinner. The major took Jemima by the arm, Prescott partnered Martha, Andrew bent his elbow for Sammie, Thomas escorted Marguerite and Charlotte trailed behind them into the dining room. Sammie ate what was before her without tasting it. She trembled when she chanced to see Jemima eyeing her with disdain. She drew her napkin to her mouth and swallowed a morsel of meat. But, at last the ordeal was over, and the ladies withdrew to the parlor so the men could finish their wine and conversation.

Sammie sat beside Marguerite on the sofa, with her skirts billowing around her limbs and her hands clasped in her lap, trying with one ear to listen to her sister, and with the other to the conversation across the room between her mother and Jemima.

The men joined the ladies once more in the parlor where Charlotte sat in her pink ribbons and black patent shoes at the pianoforte, and she played softly, creating a gentle accompaniment to the voices filtering throughout the small groupings of gathered attendees. Andrew drew to the side of the musical instrument, watching Charlotte's hands for a moment, before commenting with a smile. Moving to his aunt's side, he spoke to her with a laugh, before stilling his expression to listen in rapt attention as she extolled him on some matter or another.

Sammie's eyes followed him about the room, although with the mix of people moving to and fro, occasionally he disappeared from her vision.

"Samantha, how beautiful you look in your green." Marguerite touched her gently on the hand, pulling Sammie's attention her way. "I fear it won't become me nearly so well, when you're gone away. Mama has promised it to me."

"Thank you." Sammie turned her direction, nodded her head in a quick bow of thanks, but when she looked for Andrew again, he was gone.

"My newly betrothed." Andrew's voice caught Sammie by

surprise. Marguerite gave a sigh, her romantic heart aflutter.

"Oh, my, I thought you across the room." Sammie patted her breast to catch her breath, as she turned to the man she found so charmingly handsome.

"I was, but now I'm not. I must stay in motion, or my aunt will think you've commandeered me for the night, but I couldn't force myself to remain apart from you the entire evening. Until later." He touched her hand again, and he disappeared into the throng, only to reappear at the fireplace, joining in with the group of finely dressed men. She saw her father rap him on the shoulder and turn to Prescott. They laughed.

"Sammie, dear, may I have your ruby necklace when you go into the wilderness?"

"What? Not wear my necklace? But, Mama didn't say I couldn't take my jewels."

"What if the Indians steal them? What value would they be to the savages?" Marguerite huffed. "I know I should be frightened if I were to be going into the jungle. Charlotte will have the pearls, of course, she's younger, but I much admire the ruby on the silver cha—"

Sammie jumped when she heard a deep male voice speak in her left ear. She turned and saw Andrew beside her. She hadn't noticed him cross the room to her through the babble of voices.

Marguerite tittered and smirked behind her open fan.

"Come, my dear, I have your father's permission to speak alone with you." He guided her from the room and down the hall to her father's office.

She swept into the room, and had taken only a few steps when he turned and spoke to her. Her heart started jumping in alarm when she saw again that gleam in his eyes that she had noticed earlier.

"My dear, you are precious and so young. I fear the wilds of Kentucky will change you when the time of hardships and danger come to us. But, we must take this time to conclude our plans for the ceremony. Would Thursday be too soon? I don't want to keep the other settlers confined to their campfires beyond a reasonable length of time."

Sammie thought of her packed bags and trunks, waiting in the upstairs bedroom. "That date will be acceptable, but you must consult my parents, for they have the choice of plans in their hands, not I."

"Very well, Thursday it will be." He paused and stepped closer. "You're very beautiful; Colonel Livingston has chosen wisely. I'm told by your father that you're educated and understand the dangers of the trip."

"I've spent the last few days reading and looking at maps of Kentucky. How long do you think the journey will last?" She hoped to impress him with her knowledge, but he gave her an enchanting smile that made her heart flutter.

"Take heart, my wife; you are hardly a woman, yet we'll soon be joined in body and mind. I think it won't matter overmuch."

Amazed that he could be so blunt in his manner, she heard the door close as he slipped from the room and was gone in an instant. She remained in a daze until she heard footsteps in the hallway. She grabbed a book and plopped into the nearest chair as the door opened and her father peeked in through the slight opening.

He looked around, and not finding anyone except his daughter, he came boldly into the room.

"I had thought to see you with Andrew, but you're alone. Have you tired of the women's gossip, then? I've sent your sisters to their room and escaped the aunt's clutches for the moment. The uncle has taken a turn in the garden to smoke his pipe. Nasty habit, tobacco, but I find it enjoyable. Martha's skilled at this type of social activity, and I do enjoy the company of women at dinner parties." He looked at her closely. She calmly put her finger in the book as though to save her place and rose.

"Poor Father, how tired you must be. I admit I was vastly entertained at first but grew bored so slipped in here for a little peace and quiet. Where is Thomas? Have you sent him to bed, also? I'll take my book to my room and leave you to your own devices. Goodnight, Father."

"Wait, daughter. Don't think you can fool me with that nonsense. I saw you leave the parlor with Andrew." He looked around again. "Where's he gone? Did you settle the matter of your wedding day between you? Am I to congratulate him and send you on your way with my blessing?"

Sammie laughed and threw her arms around her father's shoulders, holding the book securely in her hand. She rose on her toes and kissed him on the cheek.

"Yes, Father dear, he's tall and handsome. I'm well pleased."

She raced up the stairs and into her room where her sisters had already donned their nightgowns and were whispering to each other in the bed. She laid the unread book on the table and asked Charlotte to come help with her gown. The girls were soon fast asleep, but she lay awake on her back long after midnight remembering the few minutes in the library with her betrothed. For a moment she had sensed animosity toward her. Did he not want the marriage between them? She tried to drive the thought from her mind, but it lingered until her eyes closed in sleep.

January 25, 1792

I begin this enterprise with a glad & grateful heart. When Father approached me with the idea of marriage, I was fearful & disappointed for I thought I would have Years before marriage. But, I am now hopeful & Cheered by my betrothal, for he is young, strong & handsome. Truly, I look forward to our future life together. Mama says my youth is a blessing & I must be thankful, for the rigors of the journey into the wilderness will demand much strength & Endurance. I spent an hour with Abigail as she and Cook tried to explain the principles of housekeeping, but my attention strayed to thoughts of my Wedding day & the lovely gown that I will wear. Mama called me to her room & said I must relinquish my jewelry, & I complied with a Cheerful heart, knowing my sisters will care for them as I do. Arthur let a squirrel into the house & it caused Havoc among the servants. The poor boy is being punished by not being allowed to ride his horse in the park for a week, A severe punishment indeed, for a boy of his Ability & skill.

— 5 —

The afternoon before the wedding, Andrew met in the Watson dining room, shut off from the rest of the house, with his four advisers, Isaac Shaw, a burly man with a balding pate and a full and bushy beard; Micah Pollard, a wiry man of no great size, with thin cheeks and tall, battered boots on his feet; Angus Fitzgerald, a man of great substance, who had invested heavily in wagons and supplies for the journey; and Ezra Collendor, the most well-dressed of the four, an individual who smelled of expensive tobacco and fine whiskey. Of the group only Shaw and Andrew had experience in the wilderness.

Major Watson had invited the men and their wives to his home so they could become acquainted with his daughter's traveling companions. No amount of begging or pleading had induced him to allow the younger daughters to attend the afternoon tea, after the debacle with Franklin Prescott and his sister-in-law, Jemima Crockett. The conversation would be much too heavy for their delicate ears.

The major gazed with a pensive look at the women gathering in the formal parlor as he retrieved the heavy, wooden doors from their hidden pockets, pulling them to, and sealing the company of men into the cavernous recess of the dining room.

The feminine group, much more decorative in their flounces and frills, included Tamara Pollard, dressed in dark gray; Bessie Fitzgerald, a slender woman who carried herself with a stiff bearing and leaned on a cane, and sported a wrinkled face, a straight nose and gray hair; and Laura Collendor, her sister, as unlike Bessie Fitzgerald in appearance as day from night, displaying plump, rosy cheeks and a double chin. There were at least a dozen years that separated them. Also in attendance was Delilah Whitesides, the wife of the blacksmith. While not dressed as elaborately, Delilah was an especial friend of Martha's, and she had invited her so she would have one friendly face among the strangers.

The afternoon started quietly enough, with tea and tiny iced cakes and dainty ham and cheese sandwiches for refreshments.

"I believe you are sisters?" Delilah asked Bessie Fitzgerald, as a tray of iced cakes made its way past. Delilah retrieved two, placing them on a doily-covered saucer of finest china with a set of gleaming silver tongs.

"Yes, we are," a quiet reply came from Laura Collendor, dressed in a large hat with a feather bobbing merrily at each turn of her head. It made quite a contrast to her dour expression in a humorous sort of way.

"Oh. La!" exclaimed the exuberant Bessie. "Everyone in society knows that we had the same father but different mothers. I was a wee small girl of three when my mother died, and four when my father married his second wife, Galla. She was a pale, weakly creature and died with the birth of my brother, Benjamin. Benjamin was drowned in the river when he was ten. Then, my father saw fit to marry again. His third wife was Beatrice, and Laura's mother. When Beatrice died, he married her younger sister, Maureen. She still lives. I have had three step-mothers. Thank goodness, or I wouldn't have Laura, my dearest and most treasured sister." Bessie tilted her head and smiled in a sugary manner at her sister, as if trying to convince the group of something she wanted them to believe.

"And you, mine." Mrs. Collendor didn't smile, but rather pursed her lips with the comment. She kept her eyes on her cake, as if it might leap up and bite her. Her feather tilted forward as if to see what its master found so engrossing on the small plate.

"I would so love to have a sister." Delilah lifted one of her cakes and bit into it, talking as she chewed. "Martha is my dearest friend, and I would trade her for no other, but a sister? You are so fortunate."

"Now, now, Delilah." Martha stood at the sideboard, having returned the plate of confections for safekeeping, and she smiled warmly at her friend. "Mrs. Fitzgerald, you must tell us of the latest in fashion. I favor the new, bright colors in ribbons. What say you?" Martha laughed lightly to show she meant the comment good-naturedly as she returned to sit by her daughter.

Mrs. Fitzgerald was attired in all black.

"I believe my sister will answer more to your taste. She finds the dark greens, purples, reds and blues of the modern woman to her taste." She said the comment with a sneer. "Why can't she wear sensible colors, as I do, I ask of her, but she insists that brighter colors bring out the joviality that the males enjoy in the company of women."

"And quite right." Mrs. Collendor's dour expression remained on her mien, in contrast to her bobbing feather. Mrs. Pollard sat quietly eating a sandwich and took no part in the conversation.

The banter continued, and Sammie remained with her mother and the other women, quietly knitting a pair of socks and taking no part in the conversation unless directly addressed. She could hear part of the men's discussion, some of it quite boisterous, yet none of it concerned her, so she let her mind drift to thoughts of her gown to be worn to the wedding. She'd gone with Jemima Crockett to the milliner's shop and stood patiently while the woman selected a veil, then had pounced on a bonnet with wax grapes on the brim.

"Look, Samantha, isn't this charming? I think you must have it."

Sammie nodded her head. She couldn't imagine where she would wear it in the wilderness, and watched with dismay as it was wrapped and paid for by the woman. When shown to her sisters, Charlotte had exclaimed over it.

"Take it then; I shan't ever wear it."

Charlotte gave her a hug and proceeded to remove the hideous grapes. Really, without the fruit it was a charming hat, she mused.

She was brought from her thoughts by loud voices in the dining room and looked at her mother. Mrs. Collendor seemed alarmed. Mother went into the kitchen and brought a pot of coffee and some refreshments for the men.

"Sammie, come help me."

"Yes, Mama." Sammie set her knitting aside and rose from her chair, smoothing her pale blue skirts as she did so.

"Carry these, child, and mind you, the men are involved in a serious discussion, and they need hear nothing from you. Follow me."

Sammie held the tray with both hands, followed her mother, and as the coffee was poured, Sammie offered the tray to each man, allowing him to make his choice as he desired. Andrew glanced at her, catching her eye, the only man to do so, and he looked away.

Sammie had hoped to smile at him, perhaps give him a kiss on the cheek. His evasive response to her presence confused her, and perhaps it embarrassed him with all his acquaintances in the room.

As the women exited the room, leaving the men to their business, the men were silent for a time. When their voices started up once again, they seemed calmer, and soon, as their words slowed, the men recognized one another by calling each other's name, and they rose to leave. The major threw wide the connecting door, and the men flooded the room with their presence.

"Wives, the afternoon draws to a close, and the morning will come calling whether we call it a night or nay." That was Collendor, and he gathered a hat from its place on the wall and withdrew a slender cigar from a pocket. He left it unlighted, but placed it in his mouth and clamped it in his teeth. The area was already darkened with previous use, giving the reasoning that this was something he was wont to do on a regular basis.

"Aye, husband, and you should be the one to speak. It's because of you we're still here." His wife gave him a look that said he should have made this call some hours before.

The women gathered their hats, gloves and cloaks, and waited, chattering all the while. Andrew gathered with the men, rather than drawing close to his betrothed. Only when Sammie stepped to him did he hesitate, giving her a quick peck on the cheek, and pushing her gently toward her mother. He knotted his brow, politely shook hands all around and left with the men.

As the door shut behind them, Sammie turned to her mother, very near to tears.

"Mama, why did Andrew leave?"

"There is so much to be done at the camp. Andrew will be busy and have no time for you. Come. Help me in the nursery."

January 28, 1792

I must hastily finish this Passage, for the Children are hovering excitedly at the door for my exit. I shall have no time to write once the Festivities begin. The day started dark & dreary with every indication of an incoming Storm, but the sky has cleared & I am Pleased that it is so. Yesterday A. seemed to be changed after the meeting in the parlor. I cannot account for it, & I dare not ask of anyone. I suppose it's nervousness at becoming a Husband, for I feel some of my own. Nonetheless, I feel we'll get off to a good start. Mother is Frantic with worry that the flowers won't arrive in time. She mentioned the difficulty of getting just the right flowers because of the winter season, & I fear my mother will be up until Morning. Oh, it's a lovely day, & I shall cherish it forever.

— 6 —

It was a magnificent wedding, held in the large rock church at the edge of town. The front area was filled with flowers, lilies, primroses, a few sprigs of greenery and snow drops; and two tall candelabras shone light into the darkened room. The guests were arranged on either side of the center aisle and whispered among themselves as the groom stood stiff and somber beside his uncle and awaited the coming of his bride. He glanced nervously at his aunt, decked in lavender with a large-brimmed hat on her gray head. She sniffed into a white lace handkerchief and whispered to her neighbor several times that she was so proud of her nephew, the frontiersman.

The preacher stood with his face toward the congregation, muttering under his whiskey-laden breath the words of the ceremony, as though he'd never presided at a wedding before. In the congregation, Franklin Prescott wore a pleased, self-satisfied expression on his face.

Suddenly the quiet cadence of the music stopped and started

again with a loud note, and the audience gasped as the bride walked down the aisle on the arm of her father, stepping tall and proud beside her. As soon as he'd left her beside her bridegroom, he took his place beside his wife and children. He gave his wife a secret smile, and she smiled back with a warning of her own.

The bride wore an ice-gray satin gown with a long train; and her upper body and face were covered with a matching veil, so that nothing was visible to the audience but the cloth of her garment and a tiny glimmer of a black shoe as she glided up the aisle. She had time to notice the disapproving stare of Jemima Crockett on the front row, and she almost stumbled in her new shoes. She saw the multitude of fresh flowers near the front of the church, and the tall white tapers of beeswax. She smiled under the veil and turned toward Andrew, who joined her at the railing.

Following sedately behind the bride were her attendants, Charlotte and Marguerite, dressed in matching rose pink dresses and broad-brimmed hats. The audience held its breath, and a cough was heard near the back of the room.

The bride stood and gazed through the heavy veil at the groom's profile. She shivered in her nervousness, hoping she didn't stumble when she was told to kneel at the altar. She smiled and, in a romantic haze, said her vows in a soft, feminine voice. She noticed, but didn't become alarmed, when her bridegroom's hand trembled at the daring move to which he was committed. He said a small prayer for forgiveness. "I'm sorry for the greed of the men," he whispered, before he kissed her.

The newly married couple left the church to the sound of the tolling of bells in the steeple and rode in a carriage donated by the bride's father to the large banquet hall where the reception was held. Sammie smiled and spoke to everyone in her quiet, shy manner; and Andrew didn't leave her side for an instant. The guests passed in a procession of smiling faces, clasping hands, encouraging hugs and kissed cheeks. They slipped quietly out the side door while the music played and the guests danced to the beat of a drum and violin.

Samantha sat on the cushioned stool in front of the dressing table in the room her husband had procured for the night. She watched her reflection in the looking glass, and her eyes moved to scan the room. She'd never eaten in a public place or spent the night in an inn before, so had no idea of the quality or extravagance it must have cost him. But, she saw the deep wine-colored drapes on the window, the gold appointments and the tall four-poster bed, and almost gasped at the decadence. She giggled and turned around, keeping her ears attuned for his approach. She walked to the drapes and felt of the soft velvet-texture and gently touched a molded lampshade. Her father was very wealthy, but even their home had no such elegant features as this room.

Her soft flannel gown caressed her feet as she moved back to the stool and sat down. Taking her seashell-handle brush in one hand, she began to brush her long dark hair, streaming down her back in soft waves. She held out her left hand and admired the wide gold band on her finger. She smiled when she recalled the way Andrew thrust it onto her finger, as though he were claiming her as his most prized possession. She frowned at the thought.

Possession? That was an odd thought for her wedding night. Surely, they would be partners in this arranged marriage. She recalled her father's face as he told her of it. What had he said? He and her mother would benefit from the match? "Oh." She laid her brush on the table and, in the dim light, looked more closely in the mirror at her face. She looked the same as last week, except for the thin plucked eyebrows that Jemima Crockett had insisted she endure. She raised a finger to run it across the surface. Already, she felt a fine, fluffy surface where the hairs would soon grow back. She opened her jar of face oil and smeared a tiny drop on the brow and rubbed it in, as the maid had instructed her, and repeated it on the other. It caused a shine on her forehead, and impatient with her vanity, she took a cloth and wiped it off. It held the faint scent of lavender.

Hark! Was that the sound of a man's footsteps outside her door? She held her breath, and slowly, as though in a dream, the handle began to turn. She jumped up, ran to the bed and threw off her wrap. She thrust the covers aside and slid in. Her heart was racing, and her breath came in gasps. But, the movement at the door stopped. She tried to relax. There was silence, and her ears strained to hear a sound, but there was none. She took a deep breath and held her hand, fingers wide-spread across her chest to calm herself. It was nothing, she tried to think. A passing fancy, come on from her tension and fear of the night ahead.

She rose to sit on the side of the bed and touched the carpet with her toes. It was soft and colorful, the pattern in a circular weave of dark maroon, rose, a bright red, royal blue and yellow; and quite lovely, she thought. The single candle on the bedside table flickered as though a breath of wind had passed through the room. She leaned over, blew it out and slipped back into the bed, bringing the covers to her chin, and smelled the stale fragrance of the smoke from the candle. Slowly, she was able to see with her night vision a crack of light from the edge of the window, and she let her mind drift to the wedding. Everything had gone so well. She giggled when she thought of her mother's tantrum when Jemima Crocket had declared she would cancel the flowers.

They had been lovely. Lilies and primroses had dominated the vases, but there were sprigs of greenery and snow drops, so delicate, and the smell was intoxicating. She had to struggle to keep her eyes open, she was so tired. She forced herself to recall the faces and the names of the people, but her mind drifted, and in the warmth of the room and the softness of the linens, she slept.

She was abruptly awakened by the feel of a man's body pressed on hers. She started to scream, but he covered her mouth with a large hand, and she could smell the aroma of sweat, tobacco and the heavy spice of a shaving soap. She wiggled to find a more comfortable position, but the man shifted, and she was crushed under his weight. With one fist around her neck, he held her bound to him, and with the other hand he lifted the hem of her gown. Her mother's admonition came to her as she smelled his breath heavy with whiskey, before he separated her legs and plunged into her secret place. The hand at her neck tightened, and she could hardly breathe as the pain sharpened, and she whimpered in distress.

"Submit!" Her mother's voice rang in her ear. "Whatever he does to your body, you must submit!" Her thoughts gave way to the roughness of his torso, and he released her neck. His hand grasped her breast and squeezed. She moaned.

"Stop! You must stop, Andrew. I cannot bear another

moment."

He continued to rise and plunge into her until her senses screamed for release. The liquor smell of his breath made her nauseous, and the pressure of his body seemed to smother her. She opened her eyes wide and felt the slick sweat on his skin, and a drop fell from his brow. She didn't know what to do with her hands. She grabbed at the cloth of the bed and held tightly. He stopped moving; and she saw his eyes, ghostly and dangerous and fierce. He lay on her until her leg began to cramp, and she felt an almost unbearable pain.

"Andrew, please, stop." She tried to move her leg, and suddenly the pressure was gone. He was gone, and she moved to relieve the pain of her leg. She saw his shadow shift as he lay on the bed on his back. He said nothing. The silence frightened her.

"Andrew?" He turned his back. "What's wrong? Did I do something to offend you?"

She could hear the heavy sound of his breathing. The pain in her leg stopped, and she moved onto her side facing him. "Andrew?"

The whisper of a voice came in the darkness, so softly that always afterward she wondered if she'd dreamed it. "I'm sorry, Samantha. Go to sleep."

Her muscles were tense, and a tear gathered at the side of her eye. One, then two, then she turned her face into the pillow and moaned with despair. She felt the bed move, and Andrew withdrew and dressed in the dark. He stood for one moment at the door, then opened it and was gone. Her tears slowly dried, and she slept.

January 29, 1792

A long grueling day has been spent in quiet contemplation of my situation. Thoughts of the happenings of last night keep me ever mindful of my mother's admonition: Whatever he does, or says, or wants; I must submit. Submit. For the moment, my heart rebels at the harsh usage of my body for his momentary pleasure, but again I can see the glow in my mother's eyes. It is my lot in life as a Woman. It is my duty. It is alright. I am alright; it is only my Fanciful heart that wants love & respect. God will take care of me, Father said. Very well; I will put my trust in Him, & continue with my duties.

— 7 —

The next few days were fraught with tension as the settlers gathered on the outskirts of town making last preparations for the trip. Some of the wagons were newly built, but others were castoffs from farms that had been hastily repaired in antici- pation of the upcoming parade of settlers heading west. The quality of the repairs was of less concern to certain sly business- men than the profit received, as few settlers ever returned to complain about shoddy merchandise or repairs. One mule had already sickened and died, creating a small panic about the quality of the animals as a whole, but the sheriff had taken the matter in hand, threatening a judgment against the farmer who had provided the animal, and the matter was resolved by the partial return of the monies due to the feed already expended on the expired beast; and a replacement animal was given in com- pensation.

Of more concern were the sacks of meal and the lack of chickens to provide eggs and meat for the traveling band. Eggs packed in straw had been bought up by the dozens, decreasing the numbers of newly-hatched chicks available for the market. Only at the last moment did a wagon load of chickens arrive from Charles City, available to the highest bidders until all were gone.

Sammie stood beside their wagon, talking to Andrew, who seemed in an expansive mood. She was pleased that he'd taken the time from his many duties to attend to her. He'd been discussing with her the intricacies of the new weapon he had purchased that morning.

Lead for shot and saltpeter for gunpowder went for a premium. Sammie paled when she learned that Andrew had spent a sum of one shilling, six pence, not counting the new musket. But there was nothing she could do, so she let it go. After all, he looked so proud and handsome showing it off to her.

"It'll keep us in game, and we'll dine well," he boasted with a grin, placing the butt of the musket on the ground and holding the muzzle at arm's length. He was dressed in a long, dark green coat, with a waistcoat of pale gray with long pants, half hidden by his blackened boots.

"You look truly the part." Sammie felt herself warm to him, certain he would take care of her and keep her safe. "How will you make the lead work in the musket? It'll have to be formed into bullets, will it not?"

"My uncle has a mold. He's donating it to my endeavor." He winked and chuckled, and Sammie knew in that look he was taking it without his uncle's knowledge. She sighed. It wasn't her affair, but something between Andrew and Franklin Prescott. She was already giving up her family. She couldn't worry about personal affairs between Andrew and his uncle.

They glanced up when they were hallowed from the front of the train. She noticed that Andrew raised the musket and was instantly alert to danger.

But it was her brother Tom riding on his bay horse to the campsite. He dismounted with a flourish and shook hands with his new brother-in-law.

"Good day, sir. I wish I were going with you. But, Papa says that I must stay and learn the fundamentals of the business. I would much rather be out hunting for grouse." He grinned. "I wonder if you and Samantha might join me in a ride. I won't have another chance to visit with my sister."

"That sounds like a fine idea. I'll saddle a horse for her, but I've no time to spare." Andrew walked to where the horses were milling about in a temporary corral. Sammie watched as he had her mare, Dinah, saddled by one of the drovers. He led it to them and handed the reins to Tom.

"Don't be gone long. She has many things to prepare for the trip. I'll bid you adieu, for I shan't see you again today." He shook hands with Tom, turned and walked away. Sammie watched as he strode to a group of men under a sycamore tree.

Tom helped her into the saddle, grumbling about the treatment of his brother-in-law. Then he gave her a pat on the hand, and climbed onto his own mount. They rode for few minutes in silence.

"Are you pleased with your husband, sister?" he asked. She was startled at the question and gazed at him blankly.

"Yes, I'm vastly pleased. He's such a kindly man, don't you agree?" She tossed her head.

Tom laughed. "I haven't had time to judge. I didn't like his relations; they seemed arrogant and proud. Come, we won't speak of such things again. We must enjoy this short time we are allowed together." They encircled the campground and watched as the drovers collected the horses, cattle, and sheep into a circle in preparation for their journey. The wagons holding the crates of chickens, rabbits and pigs were next in line. The noise and dust were tremendous, and she drew her kerchief from a pocket and covered her face.

"Ewh! I hope Andrew keeps our wagon far away from all these animals."

"You'll be right behind the pig's wagon." Tom laughed, digging his heels into the horse's flanks, and causing it to leap forward. He kept his fingers dug into its mane, holding tightly as the animal threw its head back and let out a snort of frustration.

"You'll be *in* the pig's wagon, if you're not careful. Apollo is apt to buck you right off when he tires of your silly antics." Sammie's own horse was gentle by nature. She tweaked the reins, and the beast moved forward, soon in a trot following Tom and his mount.

*****

The day of departure dawned damp and foggy; the air was cold and penetrating as the teams were hitched to the wagons and the campfires extinguished.

There were ten wagons and three carts pulled by mules, and one private enclosed carriage containing Mrs. Fitzgerald, Mrs. Collendor, and her daughter, Prissy, a shy girl of twelve years. It was driven by a dark-skinned man named Rafe, accompanied by his son, Mose, a youth of uncertain years.

Andrew was preparing his horse, strapping on the saddle and tightening the straps under its belly. He looked at her, his mouth a stern line.

"Wife, we'll be on our way, soon. Now's your time to say your good-byes. I've said my farewells to my uncle and aunt, and they are even now on their way to Baltimore." He clapped his hand on the rump, holding his hand against its flank, rubbing gently, when it snorted and turned its head.

"I hope they have a pleasant trip."

He shrugged and bent to pick up the animal's leg, and inspected the hoof, brushing at it with his hand. "It doesn't matter to me."

"How can you say that?"

"Our parting didn't go well, but that has nothing to do with you. Go, girl, and say your farewells. Once we begin our journey, likely you'll not see them again."

"Never?" Sammie teased. She couldn't imagine never. Surely there might come a time she'd return with her children, or her parents would come to visit them, even if that might be years away.

"It's very far." Andrew let out a sigh, and he stepped to the wagon and began loading a stack of crates to the side. "Go, girl, and take care of your last farewells."

Sammie tossed her skirts and turned away, unsure why Andrew was being so terse. She shrugged, making her way to her kinsmen, and she kissed her parents and brothers and sisters good-bye.

"Mama, Andrew says you'll never come to visit, but I'm sure he's wrong. Perhaps in a year or two, we'll see each other again."

"If you say so, Daughter." Her mother kissed her on the cheek and gave her a firm hug, before releasing her with red eyes.

"A hug for your Papa." Major Watson held his arms out, and he pulled her into his embrace, laughing and picking her up, and only setting her back on her feet when she complained. "I called on Prescott, but he wouldn't see me. The servant said they were in a hurry to leave. Now for your brothers and sisters. Hug them well, and give each a kind word. Perhaps you'll see them again, but perhaps not. Make this a special moment for them."

Sammie did as her father asked. She told Marguerite and Charlotte to be sure to keep their room orderly, and to always turn the broom when sweeping as to make it wear evenly. She admonished Arthur, the youngest brother, to do what Thomas said, as he was the eldest. Then, to Tom, she reminded him he must be kind to Arthur and Frederick and never insist that they do any chores Tom wasn't willing to do himself.

She promised to write when she could, then waved farewell with a smile. Her father and brother, Thomas, rode for a while before turning back to the town. Her last sight of her brother was as he raced his horse across the grass, and she heard his yell of excitement. She laughed at his antics and waved to him.

*****

Their wagon was larger than the average farmer's vehicle, topped by a gray canvas cover held in place by four metal frames. It had been soaked in linseed oil to repel water. The two front wheels were slightly smaller than the back two, but size wasn't their greater benefit. They were built with strength and hardwood for greater service. The tongue was made of hickory wood and the body of the wagon of pine. Behind the wagon came a sturdy two-wheel cart, fastened to the wagon by tongue and chains so it could be separated easily. Both were well caulked inside and out. The whole conveyance was pulled by four mules, matched in size and color.

The cart carried the tent and poles, a trunk with bedding, cooking utensils, a small barrel of saltpeter, and grain for the animals. Inside and to the back, easily reached by a couple of fold-down steps, were shelves of tinned and boxed materials, small tools such as hammers, saws, chisels, shears, lath, and a length of metal for making nails. The wagon was loaded with food supplies, household goods, a bedstead, a chest of drawers, farm equipment, and trunks of clothing and personal items. Since the move was to be a permanent one, Andrew had brought certain luxury items such as paper and pen, India ink, books, a shoe-making kit, and a mantle clock. It seemed strange to Sammie when told of the contents, that it could hold such a remarkable amount of supplies.

On the outside walls of the wagon hung a broom, an ax, two shovels, extra wheels, the plow, and several lengths of rope and chains, while underneath the wagon hung a dope pot filled to the brim with axle grease. The cart exterior contained hanging on hooks a 4x6 table board and two water barrels.

Sammie rode high on the wagon seat, her excitement dampened by the thought of never seeing her family again. She shrugged her shoulders and tossed her head; the matter was settled for all time, and she must look toward the future with hope and courage, she told herself.

She was dressed in a gray wool frock with a high white collar and cuffs. It was part of her trousseau, sewn by a middle-aged seamstress in the town. Her heavy coat was tight across the bodice and hung loosely to her black, high-buttoned boots. The boots had been specially made for her by the local cobbler to withstand the rigors of the trek ahead. Perched slightly askew on her head was a felt hat of black with a heavy veil to protect her from the dust and insects of the road. Two extra pairs of shoes were hidden in her luggage; along with the cotton stockings, gloves, handkerchiefs and undergarments her mother had deemed essential for a young lady's wardrobe. Her clothing was made for endurance rather than fashion, and she had wept when she first saw them.

Beside her sat Josiah Ferguson, the driver hired to attend to her on the first leg of their journey. He was a taciturn former rifleman in the King's Army, but decided to stay in America after the war. He would be her almost constant companion and guide through the wilderness. She could sense wildness about him. He had a strong, foreign-sounding accent, and a craggy, rough-hewed face. She could see his large, leather-bound hands as he held tightly to the reins. He smelled of tobacco and a blend of spice and wood smoke. He placed a long musket on the floor at his feet and threw a large leather satchel in the wagon behind them. He turned to her and smiled. She was surprised that he did so.

"Welcome, Mr. Ferguson. I've already said my good-byes to my family, and I'm fully prepared to begin our journey. I see you have a musket with you." When Andrew had shown her his, she'd been amused, wondering if he truly planned to use it, or if their journey was his excuse for acquiring it. This man's weapon seemed well-used, and she felt trepidation in the moment of its appearance. A shiver ran down her back.

"Don't ya worry none, lassie! Yon husband has given me the right of it; no need to fear for the wild Injuns or beasts of prey whilst I'm around. I got ten years' experience in the wilderness. I plan to keep my scalp a while longer." And, he laughed out loud and took a look over the side before spitting tobacco onto the ground beside the wagon.

"I feel relieved, Mr. Ferguson. I'll ride in a greater amount of ease with you at my side." She smiled, even as she covered her mouth with her hand. She was certain she'd like this man, even if he was old enough to be her father.

After a few hours, the excitement died down and Sammie began to doze in the warm sunshine. She was bundled in her heavy wool coat and warm blankets. The slow rumble of the wagon calmed her spirits, and she slept.

February 12, 1792

> *Our journey was almost stopped before it began as Micah Pollard, a tall, blustery man, argued with Isaac Shaw that they were taking the wrong trail. He had a paper he claimed to be a map in his hand, & his face was red & damp from his excitement. I couldn't hear the whole of the discussion, but only the parts when his voice was raised in Anger. Mr. F. later explained some of it to me. I don't think it is a good start to the journey, but will abide by the decisions that are reached by the men. I wish I had a woman companion to talk to while we travel.*

— 8 —

That first night on the trail proved a demanding and harsh one for Sammie. She stood watching while Josiah set up the tent. The sun was shining, low on the horizon, and they had stopped beside a fast-moving stream. The wind was cold against her face, and she gathered her coat more closely around and pulled her warm scarf more tightly around her ears. He unhitched the cart from the wagon and pushed it to a small clearing near the stream.

Josiah pounded the hammer onto the tent stakes, and the dust flew into his face, but he ignored it. His hat was askew and his leather gloves black with age. He moved to the second stake, and Sammie took the opportunity to look around her. She saw a woman standing beside her nearby wagon, and she decided to introduce herself. She walked toward the woman, and she looked up.

"Hello. I'm Samantha Prescott. It's a cold day, isn't it?" Then she cringed in shame, for it was such a silly question, but the woman smiled.

"Yes, it is. I realize the men want to get to the settlement early enough for the spring plowing, but I hate the cold. My name's Merlene Baumgartner, and we're from Pennsylvania. My husband won a grant for land in Kentucky." She glanced around her. "There he is, over there, with the ax in his hand. Adolf came from Prussia as a child and fought in the war. His parents were opposed to his joining with the Pennsylvanian troops, so he has left his home and hearth behind. Did your husband serve?"

"No, he's taken on the commission for Colonel Livingston, in Washington City."

Sammie noticed Adolf Baumgartner coming toward the wagon, and Merlene smiled. She turned to Sammie.

"I must begin my preparations for dinner. My husband's coming. I'll talk to you later. Come over to visit when you can; it's a pleasure to meet you."

Feeling dismissed, Sammie turned back to see that Josiah had lifted the top and sides of the tent, and it stood majestically against the darkening sky. A gust of wind caught it, and she held her breath, afraid it would fall; but it held firm. Josiah put the hammer away, took the table board off the cart wall and set it between two fallen logs for her use. Next, he took a shovel from the wall of the wagon. She moved to his side and stood nearby as he dug a trench for the fire pit. She glanced around for Andrew, but he wasn't there. She watched as other men were putting up tents. She heard the sound of hammering and the braying of mules.

She had cooked at home with the guidance of her mother or the servants, but never had she attempted to prepare a meal over an open flame, surrounded by forest, the buzz of insects and the smell of wood smoke and damp horseflesh. Her wide skirts swayed back and forth, and she was frightened that the edge would catch on fire, so she climbed into the wagon and took off her petticoats. Ah, she sighed, hoping that her silhouette didn't reach the eyes of unwelcome strangers.

"Thanks, Josiah. This means a great deal to me, you being here to provide me assistance."

"Just cook me a good meal, lassie, and that be thanks enough." He grinned. He showed her how to lay the wood in the trench properly, with tinder and twigs on the bottom, and larger sticks crisscrossing so as to leave plenty of space for the air to draw in. He had her lay two larger limbs on top, reaching to adjust one before pronouncing it perfect.

"This seems so easy." Sammie warmed with pleasure. "Do I collect fire from someone else's pit to light it?"

"No, my lass," he laughed. "We got our fire right here," and he pulled out a small bag with a flint and striker. He patiently showed her how to use the flint to start a fire. She looked around in embarrassment and saw that some of the other women were having problems, too. Thus reassured, she selected some potatoes, some corn on the cob still in their husks and a burlap-covered slab of dried beef. As she turned to take a deep skillet with a lid from the crate of utensils selected for the trip, she saw that Josiah was setting up an odd contraption over the flames.

"What an amazing device!" Sammie truly marveled. This did the same as the iron bars built into the fireplace at home. The thought brought on a pensive moment. Josiah seemed to sense her change in mood, and he began to explain.

"Mr. Prescott felt ya might need your preparations a tad

simpler. 'Tis his own design." He showed her the rudimentary hinges at the top of the legs, and the lengths of iron chain to keep the legs from spreading too far apart. He wedged the legs firmly in the ground, inserted the crossbar and put pressure on it. "Old Whitsides promised he's never made one so strong. It'll last until we get to the finish of our journey without fail, never fear."

As she turned from the cart with a pot in her hand, she saw that the fire had gone out.

"Oh, my." She put the pot on the ground, then took it up again, almost in despair, for it had dirt on the bottom. She wiped it clean with her apron, and with fear in her heart leaned down to build a new fire. She followed the driver's instructions carefully, but no sparks flew onto the twigs. She groaned. At this rate, they would never have a meal. She raised her head and searched for Josiah. He was near the mules, standing with his back to her, with a hoof raised in examination.

"Ah, Josiah, if you please. The fire's gone out." She gazed at him with soulful eyes and swatted at an insect buzzing around her ear.

"What's that, missy? The fire's gone out?"

She ducked her head and murmured, "Yes. I turned to get the cooking pot from the crate, and it's gone out. I can't make it start again."

He laughed. "No cause for alarm, darlin', try again." He walked with her to the pile of wood and knelt with the flint in his hand. "Now, watch, girl." She watched closely while he lit the fire once more. "Now, you try it." He handed her the flint and striker and stepped back.

Her hands shaking and her breath coming in shallow drafts,

she mimicked his motions until a nice steady blaze was burning brightly. He threw a couple of medium-sized logs on the pile and backed away. He stood nearby while she picked up the slab of beef and began to cut it into small pieces. She blinked several times at the smoke in her eyes, and they began to tear up. She sliced what she considered enough for three people, and laid them gently in the skillet to brown in lard. She hid the potatoes and the corn in the coals to cook, and searched for the coffee and the pot. Stumbling a bit in her haste, she went to the creek with a bucket in one hand and the coffee pot in the other and filled them both.

Setting the coffee pot into the flames and the bucket near the fire pit, she dipped some of the water with a hollowed gourd and poured it into a large bowl. She scrubbed her hands and dried them on her apron. With the potatoes and corn roasting nicely, she decided she could place the skillet on the grill. Almost immediately a sizzling sound emerged, and she covered it with the lid and went back to the box for a long-handled fork, her two wooden trenchers and cups. With all this activity, she almost forgot about Andrew, but now her eyes searched for him among the other settlers.

He was near a wagon across the open space between the campsites, talking to some men. A woman with a dark blue cloak and wide-brimmed bonnet was standing near him. Why wasn't the woman working? she wondered. A quick glance showed her place her hand on Andrew's arm and stretch to kiss him on the mouth. He thrust his head back and laughed.

The scene jarred Sammie. Andrew hadn't mentioned knowing any of the women in their company. Only a relative would feel free enough to give him a kiss. She would ask him about it later. She shrugged, certain there were many things she and Andrew would learn about each other in the days to come. With a sigh, she turned back to her preparations for the meal. She turned the meat, added onions and some flour to the pot for thickening, and some water. The steam billowed up from the pot, and she clamped the lid back on it. She took a stick and poked at a piece of log that fell out of the pile, and sparks flew into the air. The smoke burned her eyes, and she wiped them with her apron, which seemed to make them smart more. The coffee almost boiled over, and reaching for a cloth, she took it off the flame. She placed it on the table board near the fancy contraption the blacksmith had made. A quick glance around, and she saw Merlene in front of her fire, with a tall man who looked like her husband talking with her. It made the campfire cooking chores seem friendly, to know other women or men were doing the same preparations as she.

With the meat almost finished, Sammie laid out the utensils, trenchers and cups.

"Aye, girl, ya do know how to prepare a pot. My hunger's done takin' my throat by storm. Where's that husband of yours?" Josiah dropped a harness he was working on over the end of the wagon, and he knelt by the fire, lifting the lid of the deep skillet with a strong stick. Inside, the stew burbled away, with steam rising into the air.

"Earlier he was with a friend, but I haven't seen them since." She leaned toward the fire and tapped the lid of the pot with a stick of her own. "Now, now, Mr. Ferguson, you can't start yet."

They waited for Andrew, but finally, out of politeness, she and Josiah ate their meal. Without saying anything, for fear of losing her calm, Sammie handed Josiah a trencher and a spoon; and setting the heavy lid to the side, she dished out a serving for him. She pulled an ear of corn from the fire, knocking it firmly to remove the ash, and slid a section of skins from the waiting skillet.

She wanted to cry, thinking it was just as well that Andrew hadn't come, for the potato skins were dry and parched, the corn husks singed and the meat too greasy. But, the coffee was good, and Josiah thanked her.

"Ma'am, that was right good coffee."

"But not the rest." She wanted him to say otherwise, although she'd suspect him of being kind but untruthful if he said he enjoyed it.

"Ya never learn if ya don't practice. Ya got a lifetime to practice, and for me, lassie, coffee's hardest. You done mastered that. The rest'll come to ya easy." He chuckled, tipped his hat, and went to tend the mules while she cleaned the dishes.

She hesitated about leaving food out for the critters of the night, and finally dug a small hole and pitched it all in, and went into the tent to prepare for bed. There was only the glimmer of sparks from the dying embers of the cook fire and the glow of moonlight to guide her. She undressed and crawled into the bedroll, with her ears keenly attuned for the return of her husband. She began to doze, cozy in the warmth of the bed covering.

"Samantha, are you still awake?"

"I am. Where have you been?" She heard the tent fabric move, and in the dim shadows of the night, he was silhouetted against the sky for a moment, then the air darkened again.

"Remove your clothes. I wish you to perform your marital

duty."

The experience was crude and harsh, leaving Sammie bewildered. When he was finished, Andrew disappeared into the night, leaving her to organize her clothing alone.

She awakened to find him gone. She knew that he had to spend time organizing and caring for the animals and the people who'd contracted to go with them to Kentucky. The first day had been grueling and uncomfortable, and lonely, for even Josiah Ferguson hardly spoke to her. But, before long she grew accustomed to the sway and roll of the wagon, at one point walking for several miles to harden her to the time when she wouldn't be able to ride.

It was late in the night when she was awakened by Andrew coming into the shelter. She waited in silence, wondering if he wanted her. He crawled into the bed, lying still. She reached for him, but he ignored the warmth of her touch and turned his back to her. She wondered if she'd done something wrong. She was tired, though, and after a time, she felt her eyes grow heavy, and she drifted off to sleep.

She awoke the next morning to Josiah's loud cursing as he hitched the mules to the wagon. She scrambled into her dress, found her stockings and shoes and peeked timidly from the shelter. At the fire, she skimmed some dead insects from the top of the bucket and poured some water into a bowl. It was ice cold. She didn't hesitate, but washed her face and hands and dried them on her apron. She shivered in the thin early morning air. A few late stars were still out, but the pink glow of the sun was seen over the wagons. She took a stick from the ground and stirred the coals and was grateful that enough heat was radiated that she wouldn't have to struggle with the flint. Soon, she had coffee boiling and a pot of porridge on the grill. She could smell the smoke from the encircling camps and gazed with shock when she saw her husband come from a wagon across the way. She stood, aghast, then quickly grabbed a cloth and removed the coffee pot from the flames.

"Morn', missy. Appears to be a bright, sunny day ahead." Josiah frowned and wouldn't look her in the eyes. "That coffee smells good." He reached for the cloth and poured himself a cup.

Sammie felt the sting of tears but refused to let them fall. She smiled at the driver and stirred her porridge. She dared to glance across at the wagon from which Andrew had emerged and saw the same woman in a long, dark green wrapper with her hair hanging across her shoulders in long brown strands. She refused to look again but quickly ate and cleaned the trenchers and pans, while Josiah gathered her belongings together and took down the tent. Not a word was spoken until they were well on their way through the tangled brush and briars.

Sammie brooded over the event all day, unable to focus on the scenery at hand, the barking of several dogs that ran alongside the wagon, or even Josiah's kind enquiries about how she was getting along riding on the hard seat. Stopping for the midday meal was a torture, as Sammie knew the woman was nearby, and no matter where she tried to look, her eyes continually fell upon the hated conveyance. Once, Andrew rode by, and he nodded at her. She hated to think it, but he looked strong and handsome riding along. Surely nothing untoward had happened, as they were now married.

Still! He'd been coming out of her wagon! Her eyes teared

up, and she brushed at them with her hands, trying her best to be unobtrusive, as if she simply brushed at her cheeks to bring herself out of a doze.

With night falling over the camp, she walked to the wagon behind her own.

"Excuse me, Mrs. Baumgartner, if I may bother you." The woman was of a fair complexion, with her hair bound in a tight bun. Her husband was away, and Sammie felt she could speak with her without raising suspicions.

"Yes, my dear? Samantha, is it? What may I do for you, Samantha?" Merlene's sleeves were rolled to her elbows, and without looking at them, she began to unroll them as she waited on Sammie's reply. Her dress was a dark green woven plaid with white lace at the collar and, Sammie could see now, at the cuffs, too.

"I've seen a woman, but I don't know who she is. She has long, brown hair, worn down." Sammie hoped that was enough of a description. She didn't want to seem too obvious.

"Yes, Melissa Palmerton, a niece of the late Senator Logan for the state of Pennsylvania. She and her husband are on their way to claim the land he won in the bounty lottery. I suppose you haven't had the chance to be introduced yet."

"Not yet. I've heard there are many from Pennsylvania among us. Are you from the same town?" Sammie smiled as she asked.

"No, Samantha. She's from Lancaster; we're from York County, but we started this trek to Kentucky together." Her eyes darted away, as though looking for someone.

"My driver says the weather will change tomorrow. He says he can feel it in his aching bones." She laughed, hoping to

69

change the subject.

"I've not met the man. Do you say he's your driver? I'd thought him your father."

"Oh, no, ma'am. My father's safe in Alexandria, Virginia, with my mother and my brothers and sisters."

"You have a large family then?"

"Indeed I do, there are eight of us children. I'm the eldest daughter. Do you have brothers and sisters?"

"No. I'm an orphan. My father and mother died in a house fire when I was young. I was reared by my aunt, who died shortly after my marriage to Adolf."

"I'm so sorry you've lost your family." Sammie wrinkled her nose and looked around. "I've left mine behind. I see your husband coming this way. I must get back to my own campfire. Thank you for the information. Good-bye." She twirled and almost raced to the wagon, embarrassed that she'd called the woman's attention to Andrew's friends. She sat on the quilt near the fire, thinking of what her new acquaintance told her.

All was frantic activity around her as the men settled the horses and cattle for the night. The late evening sun was shining brightly through the trunks of the trees, and the leaves rustled in the wind. She could smell the camp fires and the lingering aroma of coffee and meat. She had eaten a hearty meal, for she knew she'd need the nourishment for the long trek tomorrow. She sat hunched on a fallen log, her skirts bundled around her lower limbs, and her shoulders covered with a woolen blanket. She could hear in the distance the murmurs of the other people as they settled down for the night. She flecked a flying insect from her hair and began to write.

March 3, 1792

I'm confused as to what a Marriage should be. My time with A. is nothing like my mother described. However, I've promised to love him & to meet his needs, and I endeavor to do so. Each night, A. takes out his maps & his compass & gazes with a frown on his brow at the night sky. He told me that he bought the compass in a pawn shop in Shepherdstown. The shopkeeper told him it belonged to a whaler out of New Bedford. It's a handy tool on days when the sun doesn't shine, & the stars to guide us at night. He complains that it keeps pointing in a direction other than that on his maps. According to the maps, the Cumberland River should be south of our present position, & Isaac Shaw agrees with him, but some of the other men grumble.

— 9 —

A few days into their trek across the forests and wilderness, they were forced to stop for a week by the news of the Indian scouts of a large party of hostiles ahead. The wagons were gathered closely together, lending to an intimacy among the traveling party that wasn't entirely welcome. Andrew had been off in the company of other people for much of the time, but just now he lounged on a rough blanket under a tree.

"They must know another way around. Perhaps if we traveled north or south of the savages, we could be on our way." Sammie sat on a large rock, bored. "Andrew, you've traveled this land. Have you no suggestions to offer these men?"

Andrew peered at her from under the brim of a dapper hat, although one that was showing tiredness. The edges were dirty, with sweat stains on the crown.

"This traveler has no suggestions whatsoever." He shrugged and tossed a small stone to land in the dirt.

"How can that be? You're the leader of this expedition. You

have to know." Sammie stood, kicked at what was left of the morning's fire, and crossed her arms at her waist, looking out to a great, tall butte in the distance. The heat shimmered off its ruggedness. Several large birds circled in the upwelling thermals, suggesting a meal on the hoof waited to become their lunch. Sammie could see Andrew to her side, and she was at once attracted to him, and puzzled, too. Perhaps their intimacy would return when they reached their destination. The traveling must lay as much stress on him as it seemed to offer many of their group. Arguing was ripe among several members of their troupe. At least she and Andrew were civil to one another.

Andrew sat up, and he brushed at his trousers, sending dust into the air. He cleared his throat, and when Sammie looked his way, he said, "I do have maps of this location, but they're primitive at best."

"But you must remember—"

"Don't push, Sammie. My own knowledge of this area is scanty. Men have been sent ahead to examine the situation. They'll know best what to do."

"How many men?" And why are you not with them, she wanted to ask.

"Two, with the Indian. Two with integrity and courage, Hurt said. A number of the women are using the creek to wash today. Perhaps you could join them. If you wait, there'll be no one to guard you." Andrew had a harsh look on his face, clearly wanting the subject changed from his lack of participation in the exploring party, as though he felt his lack of inclusion had been an insult to his character.

"Guard us? My word, Andrew. Why do we need guarding?" They were camped not far from the fast-flowing creek, within earshot. Surely it wasn't dangerous.

"Indians." He stood, and he cleared his throat. "I have to meet with someone. I'll be away for several hours. Josiah will be able to assist you if you need anything."

Then he was gone, leaving her alone. Josiah was not around, either. At least she would have company in the presence of the other women, and she gathered up what items she could find that needed washing, put them in the canvas bag with things already designated as soiled, and made her way towards the sounds of chattering women's voices in the distance.

At the creek, the women were able to wash the clothes and bed linens and hang them on bushes to dry. The sun was hot and piercing on their backs as they hunched over the stream and scrubbed the clothing. Sammie could see two men standing with muskets on the overhang to watch for danger. She shivered in the cool air.

"Sammie!" A familiar voice called. It was Merlene Baumgartner, with a basket of clothing at her side, and something wet in her hands. She smiled and waved.

"Merlene?" Sammie was relieved to have at least a small amount of someone's attention, someone who seemed pleased to see her, anyway.

"Bring your things this way. I have a spare rock just here. We can visit as we work." Merlene leaned to the side and patted a large, flat stone that was at the edge of a swirling set of eddies.

After several hours of tedious work, albeit work tempered by stories and occasional laughter, a rush of wind blew through the camp and dark, heavy clouds hung overhead. Sammie brought her clean clothes into the tent, although they weren't completely dry. The rain began to fall at almost the same moment the scouts returned with news of a small group of six Indians, bedraggled and begging for food. They had given them some meat and shucked corn, and they had passed on out of the area. The men continued to boast of their prowess, but Sammie ceased to listen to the gossip. She sat in the tent and lamented the dampness. Her hair was damp. Her clothes were damp, and her boots were muddy. She knew it would do no good to clean them, as the rain continued to fall, so she kept them well away from the bedding and clothing. It was a dreary night, for they couldn't build a fire in the rain. They ate some leftover parched corn and dried venison, washed down with water.

As though to make up for the delay, the sun rose hot and glowing in the sky, and they were able to spread the wet garments and bedding onto bushes to dry. Sammie sat with the women knitting socks and gossiping about the other pioneers.

With the enforced stop, Sammie was able to spend an evening with Bessie Fitzgerald and Laura Collendor and her daughter, Prissy. She seemed to be a quiet, solemn girl, who hardly ever laughed. Sammie took her handkerchief from her pocket and showed the girl how to fold the cloth to make a doll. She had often entertained her sister, Sally, with such skills, and the girl smiled at last.

"You have very pretty hair, my dear. Would you like for me to brush it for you?" The girl stared at her for a moment, clutching the handkerchief doll in her hand. She nodded and pulled her brush from a box in her trunk.

"Now, that's kind of you, Samantha, to pay attention to the girl like that. I sometimes despair over the lack of playmates for her. There seem to be several boys in the train, but no girls. Have you seen a girl among the campfires, Bessie?" The woman turned from Sammie to her sister.

"No, haven't seen a one." Bessie had taken out a deck of Tarot cards and proceeded to tell them their fortunes, which only made Laura frown, and Sammie laugh. Her eyes rose often to see Sammie slowly brushing Prissy's hair. "You've gained clever skills, tending your sisters, have you not, Samantha? I noticed your sister Charlotte has lovely curls."

"It was more like, Charlotte had the skill; she came up with ever so many ways to fix hair. I'm an amateur. Marguerite is skilled with the needle. She made a very large tapestry for the upstairs sitting room. I fear I haven't the patience to work for long with the thread." She put aside the brush, and with the dexterity she had learned at her mother's side, she began to braid the girl's hair and pinned it on her head in a crown. "There," she said. "You're a queen, Prissy. Look, Mama, your daughter's the queen of the campfires." She laughed, but Laura didn't find it so funny.

"It's all very good to fix her hair, but don't be filling her mind with such notions. She'll think herself above the other campers." Laura Collendor sniffed and rose to her feet. "It's time for us to retire. Come back again, Samantha, when you have the time." She brushed away an insect, and Sammie said her farewells and walked quietly back to the camp. Josiah was waiting, and she sensed she hadn't been alone for an instant. He put his musket away and sat by the fire.

"Goodnight, Josiah. I had a pleasant visit with my friends, but the hour's late."

"That's so, missy, I'll be seeking me own bed soon."

Sammie picked up a lighted candle he had left for her and moved into the tent. She put the candle on the floor of the tent, took out her journal and wrote of the visit with her friends and Laura's rebuke.

She heard the sound of a dog's howling as though in pain and imagined it must be caught by a wild Indian. It was only later that she found one of the settlers' dogs had come across a porcupine and was badly injured. Josiah said he'd been put down, for the quills had gotten inside his nose and mouth. She mourned for the unknown dog and unknown settler. Andrew came into the tent and sat silently looking at his maps and papers. With the heavy clouds, darkness came early, and they spread the bedding across the floor of the tent, not speaking or touching each other. Josiah, as usual when it rained, made his bed in the wagon among the boxes and barrels.

March 9, 1792

> *It has been raining intermittently for a week & the wagons roll slowly through the mud & Grime. The bottom of my skirt Drags with the heavy Weight of soil when I attempt to start a fire for the coffee & beans. It's impossible to keep dry in the damp. My feet have swollen for I dare not remove my boots except at night when in the tent. Spirits are low and Rumors are flying that we're lost, but A. gives us assurances that all is well. He spends some time with each family group, telling stories of the past & encouraging the old-timers to speak of experiences of their own.*

— 10 —

As the days grew longer, more wagons and settlers joined the party. She wondered at first about it and asked her husband, but he shrugged. It had probably been announced in the local newspapers, or told from camp to camp that he was going to Kentucky and had a wife with him. That would embolden the farmers who wanted to settle in a new area, to know that women were along, he said. Andrew welcomed the newcomers and assigned them places along the train. He set out marksmen for guards among the new men, and told them to keep a sharp lookout for either hostile animals or humans.

Among the new group of settlers was a young married woman such as herself. They met quite by chance. Sammie heard the barking of a dog, and a large mongrel broke from the line of wagons, trailing his leash behind him, with the girl chasing after it. Josiah called to the dog, and he meekly came to the man, his tail and ears back. The girl was breathless from running.

"Oh, hello. I'm Tilda. I was taking some bacon from the box, and Laddie ran away with it." She pulled on Josiah's arm. "That's my dog."

He stepped back from the animal, but stood nearby as though to protect the ladies from harm. Tilda knelt beside the hound and put her arms around him. Sammie could see the hint of tears in her eyes. She moved closer. "He's a lovely dog, such a pretty color. Did you say his name's Laddie?" Although she wanted to be included, Sammie wasn't overly fond of dogs, especially large ones, so she remained aloof, but friendly.

Tilda was dressed in a heavy wool cloak with one shiny button at the neck. Under the cloak, Sammie could see a dark green frock that hung loosely about her ankles as she knelt by the dog. Her boots were brown. Perched on her head was a black hat with a gay, lighter-green silk ribbon. Very fashionable, Sammie thought. It was most becoming and showed excellent taste. She regretted that her mother had told her to leave all her quality dresses behind since she would have no place to wear them. She smiled broadly and told the woman her name and position on the train as the wife of the organizer.

"Oh, you're the wife of Andrew Prescott? He's so handsome, isn't he? I'm traveling with my mother, Doreen Patrickson, and my grandparents. My father was awarded a land warrant for his service in the late war. My grandfather is Augustus MacGregor, the retired sea captain. We're from Philadelphia."

"And, what would a sea captain be doing so far from the sea, missy? If I might be so bold as to ask." Josiah's eyes darted from the girl to the wagons surrounding them. "You'd best be getting back, ma'am, before the captain finds ya missing."

She tossed her head defiantly. "He's a wonderful man, but very gruff and loud. You see, he's used to talking loud when giving orders to his men on board the ship." She laughed and stood up, holding the dog's leash tightly in her hand. "Yes, you're right. I must go." She curtsied.

"Thank you, sir, for rescuing the dog. Please, will you come to dinner some night, Samantha? I do so want to talk with someone of my own age." She dashed away, her skirts swishing about her as she went.

*****

A few nights later, Andrew gave her permission to visit with her new friends. He walked her to their wagon, stayed a few minutes talking to her father and grandfather, and left them. He said he'd be back in about an hour. It was a nice visit. Molly MacGreagor and Doreen Patrickson had prepared a venison stew, with wild onions and mushrooms. Molly proved to be a good cook, and she voiced her opinion in a heavy accent that America was very broad. She and her husband and Doreen had come from Scotland when Doreen was a small girl, long before the war; and he had done his part in the late conflict by providing supplies to the rag-tag colonials. Thus, he had been awarded a small parcel of land in Kentucky. Linus Patrickson was a weaver by trade. He showed Sammie some of his cloth garments. They were finely woven, and his pride in his workmanship was visible as he described it.

"The British brought sheep to Scotland many years past, but it turned out a boon for us, for the weavers have plenty of wool for the looms." He let out a big laugh, his shoulders bouncing with the exercise. He was shorter by a couple of inches than his wife and had a ruddy face, red hair and freckles. He seemed a meek man in comparison to the tall, husky sea captain, but Sammie was convinced that it was a good marriage. The dog roamed freely while they ate and sniffed at her feet. She timidly drew back.

"Don't ya be getting afeard, Mrs. Prescott, he's a tame laddie; a good sheep dog, if a body had sheep for him to tend." Sammie looked at MacGreagor with suspicion.

"'Tis the truth, ma'am, got an instinct for the wolves."

"Now, don't be filling the girl's head with your lies, 'Gustus. That hound would run away, were he to see a wolf on yon horizon." Molly laughed, and her eyes twinkled with glee.

"An unnecessary waste of food, that's what he is," Doreen Patrickson voiced her opinion.

"Now, woman, he's Tilda's pet. A girl needs something of her own to run with; you love him, too. I see you petting him at night by the fire."

The visit seemed too short for Sammie, and she reluctantly left when Andrew came for her. As they moved away, she saw Doreen Patrickson stoop to pet the dog. She laughed, and Andrew looked sharply at her. But, she didn't reveal the joke.

*****

Sammie was walking beside the wagon, swinging her stick wildly to discourage any snake that might slither around in the tall grass at her feet. Although she had boots that covered her feet and ankles, she had been told by Josiah to be cautious.

Suddenly, she was roused from her daydreams by a shout at

the front of the train. She looked up to see several riders coming over the ridge and heading toward Andrew and Isaac Shaw as they rode beside the Robert Smith wagon and its multitude of animals. She watched as Smith stopped the wagon, and the secession of movement made the cages and crates tilt to the side. Her breath caught in her throat as two of the crates fell to the ground and a flurry of chickens scattered, their multicolored feathers flying into the air. She laughed at the squawking sounds and looked up at Josiah reining in the mules. He spat over the side as he brought the mules to a stop and eased up on the reins. He shook his head from side to side and jumped from the wagon. All along the line, men were stopping and dismounting. She looked again at the group of horsemen ahead.

"What do you think has happened, Josiah?"

"Can't say, missy, but it may be they've found the river." He took off his hat and wiped his brow with a faded red kerchief. "'Course, could be Injuns." He spat again.

"Oh, my, Indians?"

"Could be, missy. The men were talking about it yesterday. Some said they'd seen tracks of men in the dirt of the creek bed." He stopped speaking as Andrew rode his horse toward their wagon.

"It's the river, Ferguson. A raft must be fashioned and will take some time. Go back a few wagons and pass the word to the other drivers. We need to bunch the large animals for the crossing. Tell Hurt and Fitzgerald, if you see them, to come to the front of the train." He turned his horse and rode at a gallop past the head of the train to the body of horses, mules, cattle and sheep. He passed Smith, frantically trying to get his chickens into an empty crate. His children were collecting the chickens; the rambunctious boys were flapping their arms and yelling, while the daughter cowered near the wagon with her woebegone mother. Sammie looked toward the front and saw the dust from the roundup of the animals. She could hear shouting and a few gun shots as they circled the herd. With nothing to do until things were settled, she climbed onto the wagon seat, laid her stick behind her and watched the show. Josiah walked toward the group of men clustered around their wagons. It wasn't long until the train began its move toward the river.

Vastly entertained, Samantha looked at the activity around the river bank; the men had decided to cross the horses, cattle, sheep and other animals first. She could see that the river was very wide and deep; along both shores there was heavy growth and a few small islands dotted the water in places near the opposite bank. There seemed to be a long, smooth beach that reached for miles. One of the settlers told her not to be nervous; the riverboat men were experienced with handling the crossing. She drew her hand to her chest and spread her fingers wide as she gazed down at the greenish-black water. The shrubs and small willows lined the banks, and she was somewhat reassured until Josiah Ferguson returned and began to curse.

"Oh, Mr. Ferguson, what's wrong?"

"Don't fret, missy, I been thinkin' of the last big river I crossed. 'Twus a fearsome ride down the rapids to the bottom of the hill. There, one of the teams balked at the exit from the raft, and the wagon was overturned."

"Oh, how horrible. Was anyone hurt?"

"Nah, lass, but 'twus a sight to behold how the mules bellowed and pushed to find footin', and the men scramblin' to catch the barrels and boxes as they tumbled end over end into the water and disappeared from sight in the muddy depths. The poor Wider Jameson lost everything and had to join forces with another couple. They left her at the fort, and I don't justly know what happened to her after that." He spit a stream of tobacco at the ground and sighed.

He became silent, and Samantha gazed at the first wagon to gain access to the raft. It was piled high with crates of chickens and carried some cages with rabbits. Tied securely in the back were a sow and six piglets. They belonged to the Robert Smith family, and Andrew had assured her that once they arrived at their destination, he would buy a couple for them. It would be the start of some hams and sausage dinners. As she watched, she held her breath. The mules were coaxed aboard first, one pulling to the side and threatening to overturn the entire assemblage. A whip cracked in the air, threats and commands were yelled, and with a bray of acquiescence, the stubborn animals lurched forward, dragging the wagon after them. Smith's wife let out a cry of alarm and reached for her children to comfort them, but the younger Smiths were hooting with the joy of it all, and called their animals by name and encouraged them on. The front wheels of the wagon caught on the edge of the raft, and it seemed for a moment that all the men's efforts would be lost, before the conveyance leaped past the broken line between craft and shore, and with a precarious amount of swaying household goods, the wooden land yacht made its way aboard, jerking riotously as it bumped over the curved surface of each log making up the massive raft.

Samantha's heart pounded in tense apprehension, as if she herself were aboard the sturdily built raft. As the men began to pull on the ropes, they set up a chant, two or three tugging as one in a repeated rhythm of interconnected cooperativeness that made them seem as a single entity. It was a sight of unparalleled cohesiveness among the traveling party, and Samantha knew it would surely bond them in their intents and purposes for all time. The river waters swirled around the raft, creating a pattern of dimpled waters and twisting eddies. Once, a fish leaped, nearly landing on the raft. The youngest Smith whooped. Even from the distance, Samantha could hear the boy's pleading cry to be allowed to bait a hook and catch their dinner. His mother was clearly in tears, sobbing and sending up prayers for their safe passage. She pulled the boy to her, silencing his elation in the ample folds of her bosom in an attempt to comfort herself, and sending a wave of laughter through the men wrenching the raft across the river. The only true diversion was a log that bobbed in the water, coming from upstream and heading directly toward the hapless watercraft. Sammie held her breath, considered that Mrs. Smith's worries might be validated and wondered if God would, indeed, allow them safe passage. She found she needn't have worried, as the lead man lifted a long pole and prodded the log until it made its way past the end of the raft, twirling, disappearing for a short time, then reappearing a short distance downriver and moving rapidly out of sight. To Sammie's relief, the raft glided safely to the far shore. The scene at the beginning was repeated, although with much more enthusiasm by the mules, for they leaped for the safety of the land as if they had been on their way to the underworld and were now given reprieve. The wagon lurched after them, twisting horribly as it dropped off the raft, twisting the floating conveyance sideways, and landing the rear wagon wheels in the water, before vaulting bravely to dry land. With a yell of triumph and encouragement to the mules, the men pulled the animals to a stop near a large boulder.

Sammie let go her breath and turned to see Josiah laughing at her. She ducked her head in shame.

"Well, that seems safe enough. I'll go to see how Tilda Creasy is doing." She ran to the back of the wagon train where her new acquaintance was standing with her husband and mother, Mrs. Patrickson. Tilda was in a similar situation to Sammie, and she'd felt a kinship with her from the first word the other woman had spoken. She and her new husband were off to make a new life for themselves, just as Sammie and Andrew were. Sammie didn't know what she thought about having her mother along. It would perhaps be a good thing, if she didn't feel the need to interfere overmuch. Samantha knew her own mother would never abide such rigors as this trip would surely entail, and besides, there were her younger siblings to think of.

"Oh, Tilda, you should have been at the front to see the first raft crossing. At first I wondered if all their things would tumble into the water, but there was nothing to worry about. I do believe we'll be safe enough. The river seems so calm and the men are experienced, my driver says."

Sammie knelt and rubbed the woman's brown pup behind the ears, laughing when he brushed her hand with his tongue. "Be sure to keep Laddie tied up securely. He might float down the river if he decides to jump in."

"Do you think so?" Tilda seemed distressed.

"I do not think so. I shouldn't have teased. There's nothing to fear. We'll safely reach the other side, I'm sure." Sammie smiled as she stood to show she'd been teasing about her friend's pet.

"I fear it's not so, my dear. I've crossed large rivers before, and the water may seem calm on the surface, but there are sunken logs and roots to snarl the ropes and chains. You mark my words, nothing good will come of this day." Mrs. Patrickson turned and walked away, and Samantha sighed at the pessimism. She saw tears form in Tilda's eyes and took her hand and tried to reassure her.

"Never mind, Tilda, dear. We're in good hands. I have to get back to my own wagon; I believe we'll cross the fifth in line, and I'd best be ready." She tossed her head and smiled. "I'll see you on the other side." And with a hug, she left her friend and slowly moved along the line of vehicles to her own patiently waiting driver. Sure enough, the second and third wagons had crossed and were lined on the far shore. She held her hand over her eyes, the better to see, and saw her husband ride his horse beside one of the drovers to speak to him. He gestured to the men to hasten farther away from the banks so the others would have more room to congregate on the soft, sandy banks.

She grinned as she saw him look in her direction. She knew he wouldn't be able to see her among the throng, but she raised her arm to wave and surprisingly, he waved back. She turned around, pleased by the gesture, and heard some men arguing about whether the women and children should be roped to the wagon wheels while they crossed. Jess Bond said they would be safer, but Natalie Foresome objected.

"I will not be tied down like an animal. What if the raft sinks and I'm drawn under by the current? At least if I'm free of the bonds, I'll be able to swim away from the wagon."

"But, the river is too deep and swift. You can't swim that far, ma'am. You did watch the previous wagons, I presume. There's some danger in coaxing the animals onto the wagon, and just as much exiting on the other side."

"She's right, Jess. I suppose most of the women, and certainly the young ones, can't swim, but at least they would have a chance to break free if they aren't tied to the wheels."

The conversation might have continued on, but Josiah Ferguson came for her as their team was ready to board the raft. She walked as calmly as she could to the wagon, but her heart was beating rapidly and her hands began to curl into fists. She wouldn't be tied down. She would not! She was determined that if the wagon rolled off the raft, she would not be tied to it.

"Josiah, I will not be tied to the wagon wheel." She gazed at him fiercely.

"What, missy? I don't understand. Who said you'd be tied to the wagon wheel? I'll be close by if the raft should be tossed. I swim very well. Donna you fret about it."

"Back there, they said the women and children should be tied. I cannot believe that's the best solution."

"Nay, 'tis a foolish notion, but we donna have time to worry. Here we be. Just you hang on to me, missy, you'll land safely across." And, he winked and spat his tobacco juice on the ground.

Unlike the first wagon, it was decided that running the wagons onto the raft without people aboard was better, and the family members could then board safely and stand beside their vehicles on the ride across the swirling waters. Dust swirled as the men called loudly, directing the mules, some of which were balking, showing the whites of their eyes, and braying with a loud commotion. One man thought to tie a bandana over the animals' eyes, quieting the commotion, saying that if the noise and disturbance spread to the entire wagon train, they would soon get no one across. Sammie considered his idea a boon, although she remained content not to ride on the wagon as it made its torturous entry onto its perilous home over the watery road ahead of them.

The men had fashioned a brace of heavy logs to make a raft for the heavy wagons and carts. The ends were ragged with ax marks, white against the brown bark making up the surface of the raft. Thick ropes darkened with river water twisted between the logs, strapping them firmly together. Sammie considered it a wonder that the wagon wheels made it aboard at all. She shivered to think of riding aboard as Mrs. Smith had been. Surely she would have screamed in terror, also. She was chosen to ride on one of the rafts along with Mr. Ferguson and two other ladies, Mrs. Fitzgerald, Mrs. Collendor, and Mrs. Collendor's daughter, Prissy.

Reassured, she smiled valiantly at Prissy and stepped lively onto the raft after the wagon and cart carrying her precious supplies and tent were secure. She was followed by the other ladies and Josiah. She turned her face defiantly to the opposite shore and took a deep breath. She felt the shaky movement as the raft began to leave the firm ground and settle onto the surface of the water. She didn't look back but watched with bated breath and excitement as the ropes pulled the raft into deeper water. The whirling water encircled them, and the water seeped up between the logs and flowed over the surface.

She kept her eyes on the waves breaking across the logs and

watched in fascination as the water crept to the edge of her boots. She stood like a stone, and felt the gentle breeze and a slight mist from the water. Oh, it was wonderful! she thought. Nothing was like it in the world. Her pulse quickened when she saw the men and animals lined on the opposite shore. She heard a screech and looked up quickly to see a hawk, his wings spread wide, soaring in the sky. She laughed out loud, it was so fine.

She felt the presence of Josiah Ferguson near her, and she turned to him. He had a gleam in his eyes, and she knew he felt the same joy as she did. She laughed, and he laughed with her. She watched the other ladies and smiled. Then he sobered as the raft came near the bank and disaster almost overtook them. She gasped when the guide rope broke and they began to be tossed here and there like a ship without an anchor. She clung with fear to the side of the wagon wheel and watched as one of the strangers swam to their rescue. With the strength of his long arms, he grabbed the rope and was able to pull them to safety.

"Sam." She heard her name called, and she looked to see Andrew dismount from his horse to welcome her.

"Andrew! You should have been with us. Riding across the river was so very exciting, although I don't suppose everyone was as thrilled as I."

"Come. I'll help you disembark." As the ride across the river came to an end, he held out his hand, and she grasped it strongly. He gave her a quick hug and turned to see the wagon hitched and drawn from the raft. She looked at the people lined on the far bank and could just make out the form of her friend Tilda and her mother. It appeared that the argument was over, for none of the women or children were tied to the wagon wheels. She found a small boulder on which to sit and watched two more crossings before Josiah told her they must board the wagon and head west. She climbed aboard the wagon and was grateful for the warmth and safety of the ground.

A few yards beyond the river bank, they were stopped dead by a wall of greenery. The animals were bunched together, milling about seemingly without purpose, while the wagons began to circle, the animals snorting and kicking their traces.

It was a heavy thicket, the trees so plentiful, it would be impossible to pass. Andrew consulted his maps and discussed the situation with Isaac Shaw and Angus Fitzgerald. According to the map, it was called Bryant's Path. Beyond about seventy-five yards, there was marked "Salt Lick." They were eager to forge ahead, so Andrew assigned two men to explore and hack a trail. Four other men were assigned to go along the river bank to look for signs of humans traveling along the path.

There was a great shout, and Sammie looked up to see Sanford Kendall come running along the sandy beach, yelling that he had found it. Tilda's large brown dog broke away from the wagons and raced toward the man, jumping on him relentlessly. He was hard pressed to escape the dog, but several of the men rushed to his assistance, and he was able to explain that he had found a clearly marked trail about fifteen yards to the south of their current position. It was thick and heavy with brush and briars but clearly a marked trail. There was no evidence that any large number of wagons had ever crossed the path.

The news was considered by the authorities, and the dog tied securely to his wagon, so as not to disturb the assembly further. Josiah went to the men and huddled at the edge to gain information for Sammie. The women stood by, anxiously waiting.

Josiah came toward them, slowly shaking his head. He grinned when he saw Sammie, standing with Bessie Fitzgerald, Doreen Patrickson, young Prissy and Tilda.

"'Tis nothing to get overexcited about, missy. We just need to remain here while the men hack a trail through."

"But is it possible?" Doreen asked; her body stiff, her lips pursed and holding her parasol high in the air.

"Oh, surely, 'tis possible, will take some time. May as well collect yore sewing needles and sit a spell." And with that, he marched to the mules and tended to their needs.

"Well, such a to-do about nothing, I say." And Mrs. Patrickson strode to her wagon, her shoulders huffed and the parasol tilted at an odd angle. Bessie gasped and trotted after her, leaning heavily on her cane.

Sammie smiled and turned to her friend. "It'll be fine to sit for a while, don't you think, Tilda? You better see if Laddie needs water."

"Oh, yes, I must go see if Laddie is alright." And, she bounded away, her skirts twirling around her, causing the dust to rise at her feet.

Sammie continued to watch the men gathered in the circle. They seemed to be discussing what was best to be done. Soon, Andrew broke from the crowd and came to tell her their decision.

"I think we'll camp here for a few days, Sam. The men will have to make a path through the thicket. Kendall says the path is marked with x's on the tree trunks, but it's for certain sure, no large amount of wagons have attempted the trail. I've chosen four men to chop their way through the tangle of vines and trees." He unfolded his map and laid it against the side of the wagon. "See. We're a few yards off the route, but it's clear Kendall has found the right marks." He pointed to a slight, faded notation at the bottom of the map. "The trouble is that the vegetation is so heavy that the marks were hard to make out from the river. We'll stay here for the time being." He shook his head in frustration. "It may take days to make it through this tangle, but I'll see that we get through as quickly as possible. Watch the rations carefully. Water is plentiful, but the food will be scarce if we have to tarry long." He looked around the perimeter. "That looks like a good spot to park, away from the water should it rise, but a good distance from the forest." And, with that vocal advice, he disappeared among the men walking toward the marked path, talking and gesturing wildly.

"Climb on board, missy, and I'll move the wagon a ways. Looks like we're here for the night."

Sammie did as he asked and climbed into the wagon. With his arms straining at the reins, Josiah guided the mules to the spot pointed out by Andrew, and there he proceeded to make camp. The mules were unhitched and tied securely where they could nibble on the grassy verge of the sandy beach. The cart was unhooked from the wagon and pulled around for her convenience. She started gathering firewood.

"Don't go far, missy. Remember the poison sumac vines." Josiah shouted, and she responded with a wave. She chose only those limbs and twigs that she could see were not near any greenery. She piled her arms high with the timber and dumped it in a likely spot for a fire. She glanced around and saw that the other wagon drivers had taken places of their own choosing. She was pleased to see the bright, shiny brown coat of Tilda's dog and knew her friend was nearby. Abe Creasy was chosen as one of the men to hack through the wilderness. As she began to start a fire with the flint and striker, she could see that Molly MacGreger had taken out her colorful wool bag and was busily knitting while the others prepared for nightfall.

It was fortunate that the camp was far enough away from the clearing, for soon a dark black smoke arose from the burning of brush and vines. It would have been difficult for the women to breathe and keep their clothing clean in the process. The tall trees were felled and set aside, while a couple of the men took draw knives and scaled the smaller limbs and bark from the trunks. News came back that night with Abe Creasy and others that the mules were used to haul the logs to a clearing after it was open, and if possible would be used for repairs for wagons or sawed into lumber.

The days were slow moving for the ladies, remaining at camp. They heard rumors and tales of the heavy brush and vines being chopped and burned. The smell of smoke was ever present, especially when the wind shifted from the west. Sammie was sitting on a stump, her knitting in her lap, talking quietly to Tilda, when she thought she saw a hostile face in the bushes across the circle near Mrs. Fitzgerald.

The dog lay on the ground asleep near his mistress. Suddenly, he rose, frantically barking, and trying to break away from his rope restraint. Mrs. Fitzgerald must have seen the face in the bushes, too, for she commenced to scream. Josiah raced toward them with his musket in hand.

"Look, Josiah, it's a man." He needed no more explanation than that. Yelling at some other men, who had heard the dog's agitated barking, they took off at a run after the man in the bushes. The ladies put away their sewing bags and huddled together in a group. Each sound of shouting or shooting brought new alarm. Soon, Josiah returned, and Sammie felt more comfortable with him around. He was almost breathless with running, and his face damp from sweat. He took out a kerchief from his pocket and wiped his brow.

"I'm sorry, lassie. He got away from us. The other men seem to think he may be a scout for a tribe or maybe the militia. He must have been mighty surprised to see white females sewin' in the afternoon." It was meant as a joke, but Mrs. Patrickson huffed and walked away, with Tilda holding tightly to the dog's leash and following meekly behind her.

Early the next morning, as she peered from her tent, she saw a deer standing not two feet from the entrance. The graceful creature was nibbling on some green foliage, her ears twitching at the buzzing flies. Sammie dared not breathe or make a sound. She heard a noise from the wagon, and Josiah came from behind it. The deer scampered quickly away into the dense forest.

"Oh, did you see her, Josiah? Wasn't she lovely?"

"Lovely is right missy, but I reckon she'd made a good venison stew, if'n I'd had my musket ready."

Sammie gasped in shock, but then she detected the gleam of laughter in his eyes and sighed. She chastised him, "Well, I think she was beautiful."

"'Tis true, my girl, she was, at that." He rolled up his sleeves and began to rake the spent coals and ash from the fire pit in order to prepare for breakfast. When he had finished, he left her to her chores and went to fetch a pail of water.

March 25, 1792

Poor Thos Hurt was brought down by a horrible Rash from the poison sumac among the vines they were cutting, J. said. His arms & chest were raw & red & his Eyes almost closed from the contact. He kept to his tent & the ladies were busy discussing the best remedy for the Affliction. Bessie said clean axle grease was the thing for it, but Doreen said that sulfur powder was the more efficient for taking out the poison. I cannot say which is best, but A. has ordered me not to leave the wagon until the way is Clear. I sit now with pen in hand & smell the smoke from the burning bushes. One of the ladies declared that even the Smoke carried the Poison aloft into the sky, & I have covered my face with a cloth in case she is right. I fear for the other men, who have been exposed to the Dreadful rash.

— 11 —

The campsite slowly settled into its routine, and Josiah went about his business. Sammie, her heart racing, wished her husband was there, but he was as usual with the men. The monotonous days lingered on, but eventually the work was done, and the wagons were able to roll again through the new road. It was bumpy in places, and Sammie hung on tightly to the wagon. The path was narrow, but there was no danger that Josiah could see; so she walked part of the way. The wagons lined up in single file, and the sounds of mules braying, their harnesses jangling, and the driver's curses had become familiar to the young matron as she rambled along, a smooth, slightly crooked stick in her hand to ward off snakes or other small critters. She didn't see Tilda or the other ladies, as they were riding a few wagons behind. She thought once she caught a glimpse of Andrew on his chestnut stallion, but the dust was so heavy she might have been mistaken. She shrugged and continued on, her boots kicking up dust from the high grass.

It wasn't far, about seventy-five yards to the open meadow and the salt lick. They spent a day cutting squares of salt for the use of each family group and were on their way across the ridges and valleys. Another large river was crossed, and Sammie was now more settled in her mind with the experience from the first one. The animals and wagons crossed safely, and the trip continued without incident.

At Sammie's request, Andrew had spoken with Tilda Creasy's husband, and as the women had become acquaintances and even begun to consider themselves friends, the men accepted it would be in their best interests to accommodate their women in this small way. Besides, what harm could it do to encourage cooperation between their respective families? Now their wagons kept within sight of one another.

As the days slowly passed in succession, the people began to look forward to the arrival at Harrodsburg. The days were monotonous but not overly long, for it was still spring. One morning she awakened, and there was frost on the ground. It was lovely, sparkling in the early sunshine, but she ducked back into the tent and found her mittens and scarf and tied it tightly around her ears. It took a while to get the fire started, but its heat was welcome. She felt, rather than saw her husband come from behind her.

"Good morning," she said.

Andrew ignored her cheerful greeting and stood above the fire for a moment warming his gloved hands. "I think we'll come to the settlement soon. I've sent out two scouts in advance to see if they can spot it. Hurry with breakfast; I need to check one of the wagons. Isaac said he thought it would lose a wheel." He walked away, and Sammie ground her teeth in frustration.

She quickly sliced some bacon and put a pot of porridge on to cook. She stamped her foot.

"I hate porridge. Oh, what I wouldn't give for some of Mama's delicious sweet raisin pudding, with slotted cream and maple syrup."

"Well, missy, I'd sure like some of my mammy's corn bread stuffin' and a big fat turkey gobbler, but a person got to make do." Josiah grinned at her and spit his tobacco on the ground.

She laughed. "If you'd go and shoot that gobbler, I'd cook it for you. I think tomorrow I'll fry some potatoes and onions for a change." She spoke defiantly, and he walked toward the mules, laughing.

March 27, 1792

T. has become a great comfort to me. The Days grow long riding on the trail. Great swathes of dust rise into the air, & it seems it's all that I can see for hours on end. I wonder how long her husband will continue to get along amicably with Mrs. P. Three days ago, there was a Disagreement among them about the amount of lard used to fry the frog legs Abe had captured from the creek just passed. T. was all for tossing the used lard aside, & her mother insisted that it could be reused, & it was Wasteful to cast aside something so valuable so Carelessly. T.'s husband supported his wife, naturally, but I agreed with Mrs. P. Nothing can be Wasted, or we may indeed run out of adequate supplies before our journey is complete.

*****

By the last week in March, there were twenty wagons, over one hundred horses and mules, seventy-five sheep and sixty-two cattle with them. In addition, there were milk cows, chickens, hogs and goats. Sammie felt a sense of pride that her husband was the leader and guide. She watched him talking to the men, laughing with the women, picking up a small child and carrying him on his shoulders, and she wondered at the strength and courage of the man. It was only during the dreadful nights, when he was lying beside her, that she acknowledged that her marriage was a mistake. She could see clearly now that he didn't want her; had been forced into the marriage by her father's greed and Colonel Livingston's avarice.

Over and over in her mind, Sammie saw the parlor of her father's home on the occasion when Jemima Crockett looked on her with such scorn and censure. She could see the quiet acceptance in the eyes of his uncle Franklin Prescott, as he listened to her father's tales of politics and past courtroom drama. They had come to guarantee that the marriage take place. What kind of hold did they have over Andrew, she wondered? Would he be free now from their influence, or was he bound to them until he cleared the land and had a fort built? Sammie sat near the campfire and watched the flames bite through the logs and the sparks fly into the air. She made a secret vow with herself that no matter what the future held, she would remain cheerful against the odds; she would support her husband as he struggled to escape the bonds that held him to her father, Colonel Livingston and his obligations to them.

Without warning, while she sat by the fire, a loud cry of alarm was heard, and before she could stumble to her feet, a wagon rushed passed her. She could see the frightened faces of the women as they were jostled and tossed about in the wagon. It was young Todd Weatherspoon, driving at an alarming clip. Sammie gazed in awe as not twenty yards from the tent opening, the wagon overturned, and all were thrown out of it. The bags and barrels went flying into the air, with a cloud of white flour, salt and cornmeal spraying the air, then coating the ground like snow.

"My word! Andrew! Andrew!" Sammie called, unable to find him. She gathered her skirts and started that way, only to be overtaken by others who seemed more assured of what to do.

One of the settlers ran to unhitch the poor, struggling animals. Lizzie Weatherspoon lay still, while Mrs. Grissom, her mother, writhed and moaned in pain.

Seeing the two women unattended, Sammie ran to them, but was held back by the crowd gathered around.

"Let me through, please. Please." She pushed at shoulders and arms. She could see blood on Lizzie's face and almost retched at the sight. "Please, you must let me through to assist."

The gathered throng wouldn't relent, however, and she was prevented from approaching closer. Andrew and Isaac Shaw came running and took charge of the scene. She had never seen death so close at hand, and such a terrible tragedy. The whole camp was somber as they moved around the campfires; the gossip was rampant among the pioneers. Josiah just shrugged when Sammie tried to get him to talk to her about the accident. Andrew stayed away until almost midnight, and he made his way quietly through the camp in the darkness. At one point, he drew near to her.

"Are you awake, Sammie?

"Yes. I can't sleep for thinking of poor Lizzie. Does anyone know what happened?"

He whispered, "One of the harness straps broke, and Todd isn't to blame. We'll take two days for the funeral and for Todd and Mrs. Grissom to heal from their wounds. Go to sleep, for there's nothing to be done about it otherwise."

She lay almost frightened beside him as he seemed restless. Her thoughts were filled with the yells of fright, the sounds of the snorting animals as the wildly careening wagon flew by, and her last sight of Lizzie Weatherspoon in the wagon, her hair flying, and a look of uncomprehending surprise on her face. She wondered if Lizzie had felt afraid, and if she'd suspected her wild ride would be her last ever. She shivered in the dark, but finally drifted off to sleep.

April 2, 1792

The cooking fires are slowly dying as I sit on the ground with pen & paper in hand. I can barely write for the Tragedy that has transpired. The people are subdued & the children have been put to bed early, as we all contemplate the sadness of the moment. Two lonely mounds of newly turned sod appear to the left of the camp, a sad commentary on what can happen when a man grows careless in his habits. The breeze picked up and blew a piece of paper across the newly turned earth. The paper caught on a clump of soil, and it seemed as if angel wings hovered over the grave for a time, before it whipped away and was gone. J. said he should have noticed the frayed harness strap, but I cannot blame Weatherspoon as others have done this day, for he has suffered a great loss. His wife, only nineteen years old, died almost instantly & his mother-in-law during the long night just past. I wanted to speak to someone because of it to ease my own Misgiving over not being able to offer solace but didn't know his wife well, and consoled myself it was better for A. to deal with it. Still, to be alive then gone so suddenly. Will others be lost along the way? How many will wish they had never embarked on our Journey? Mariah Philips was overheard to say that W. should be left behind, but A. has decided the whole was an accident and we will move on tomorrow with the repaired wagon & W., his leg in splints. A kindly farmer named Silverton has agreed to take him aboard his own vehicle until he mends. The contents of his wagon that have survived the accident & the wagon itself have been sold to those who could afford to buy such items of necessity. He will take the money, A. said, and return to Virg.

— 12 —

As the days grew longer, and the sun warm on their backs, the settlers shed their heavy coats and scarves and gloves. Sammie had lost weight but was gaining muscle in exchange. She now could walk most of the day without tiring.

She was standing over a pot of rabbit stew with vegetables and dumplings, when she heard a loud sound of shouting from the forest about three wagons ahead. She took a cloth, pulled the handle of the pot away from the spit and laid it on the ground; then ran to see what the shouting was about.

She hovered close to the edge of the crowd. From what she could make out from the moans of Ed Hicks, who was bare-chested, with his head covered with his bloody shirt, and Fountain Principle's explanation: he, Hicks and Otis Gerrard had set out around noon to find wild game. They had been set upon by a group of wild Indians with tomahawks and lances. One man, dressed only in a breechcloth and feathers, whacked Hicks over the head, and drawing a knife from a pouch on his shoulder, tried to scalp him. Two men surrounded Gerrard and brought him to his knees; while Principle was able to raise his musket and shoot the man with Hicks. Hicks and Principle were able to make their escape and ran towards the camp; but they feared that Gerrard was dead.

Retta Gerrard broke out in loud cries of anguish, and Samantha and Merlene led her away to her wagon. Looking back at the scene, she saw that her husband and several other men were discussing whether to follow the trail of the Indians or to look for Gerrard. Shaw volunteered to lead the party if Hicks would show him where the incident happened. She didn't have a chance to hear the outcome until the next morning. Andrew came to her at breakfast, his hat held contritely in his hands, his head down. He watched her at the fire, working the edge of her hoecakes.

"It's been decided to hold off today before moving on, so there'll be time for sorting supplies, or even visiting the river if you've got things to wash." He glanced at the folded bedding visible inside the wagon. "Maybe air the bedding out; that would be good."

"Not leaving?" As the hoecakes began to sizzle loudly, Sam took the handle of the skillet with the hem of her skirt and moved it off the center of the fire. She looked hard at her husband. "Is this about Retta's husband? Is he severely injured?"

"More than that." He twisted his cap as if saying it made it true. "We found him dead, his body mutilated." He looked away, his expression stoic and his brow furrowed.

Samantha gagged, putting an arm to her mouth, and turning away. She didn't want to know more, not with weeks, still, of traveling before them.

"Should I go to Retta to comfort her?" She fought tears, thinking of what the grieving woman must be going through. She knelt and turned the cakes for something to busy herself with.

"Later, perhaps. Several others are with her now. I must go as we decide what to do in remembrance. Some of us feel it would be only right, and, well, we're going to do it."

"Don't you want to eat? It's about ready."

"No, not now; maybe later when we've more time.

Samantha brushed her eyes with her sleeve as Andrew walked away, wondering why she'd agreed to this venture into the wilderness. It was a horrible way to die, and she imagined it happening to her. To Andrew. The very idea was insurmountable. She looked at the hoecakes. Her appetite had left her, and she wrapped them in a clean cloth for later.

*****

The children took the day as a sort of holiday, not being on the trail and allowed to play together. Samantha noted the parents who kept closer watch than usual, herding the young'uns in when they strayed too far. No Indians were seen, a small consolation, as the fear of them likely would have brought the train to a state of panic. She took the opportunity to stitch some loose seams in one of Andrew's shirts, brush sand from the floor of the tent and visit with two or three neighboring families for an hour in the afternoon. By the time the horizon glowed orange with the setting sun, and the evening's meal of venison and baked potatoes, still hot from the bed of coals, was laid out, the men had discussed the finding of the body for hours.

Samantha scooped potatoes and meat onto wooden trenchers; glancing at the men sitting on rocks with Andrew. Josiah had joined them, his face pinched with sorrow and regret over the tragedy. Bigger Houghton, who had been a blacksmith in Baltimore, and had the broad girth to prove it, jabbed a meaty finger Andrew's direction.

"Told Macie this would happen. No one's done a proper job of removing the red men from these parts. Not since St. Clair's defeat on the Wabash in '91. And where there's Shawnees or Delawares, there's killing. No way around that."

"Now, Bigger," Andrew cautioned. "There's no way to remove them all, and you know it. The government gave them certain areas for their villages. It's probably a band of renegades out looking for meat just like our men were doing"

"Done thought the warrior tribes moved across the Ohio. 'Twus one reason I agreed on this trip." Josiah seemed confused, the British accent in his voice unmistakable.

"He's right. Most have, but there's some what don't want to move. Claim this has been their home since the beginning of time." Red Masters, a thin rake of a man, with stringy hair and a scraggly beard, the very opposite of Houghton, drawled in a whiney-sounding tone. "Hear tell of Injuns eatin' white men. Hear tell they got a taste for white flesh. We better bury Gerrard deep, or they'll dig him up and cook him over a fire."

Samantha felt a chill run down her back, and she wished they'd stop talking. They'd be scaring the children with talk of this sort. In the distance, shovels clanked. There were two lanterns, but the orange sky, with red and golden streaks of clouds against the horizon, revealed the scene clearly. It was the dead man's grave. Closer in, by a campfire, Isaac Shaw was burning something onto a board, probably the name and date to be placed at the head of the grave.

A hound barked, and Samantha jumped, startled at the closeness of the sound. It was as if an Indian was canvassing the camp in the growing twilight, and nowhere was safe. Then she heard a child's voice, "Boomer! Come here, Boomer, boy," and she breathed easier.

Andrew finished his conversation with Houghton and Masters, wishing them farewell, and he moved to a rock closer to Samantha. Josiah wandered off to see about the animals.

"There'll be a funeral before long." He pointed off the other direction to where several women were gathered, with a man and a couple of small children. One woman with her head down being comforted by a second looked like Retta Gerrard.

"I'd like to go." Samantha handed Andrew his trencher and poured a tin of water from the cistern in the wagon. "If you think I could, that is."

"Certainly, if you want." Mosquitoes buzzed, drawn to the light of the fire, and he brushed them from his face. Taking a utensil from Sammie, he speared a slice of meat and bit it, tearing off the end before chewing.

Samantha ate silently, gazing into the light. Nearby, Micah Pollard began reading to his children from the Good Book, his thin lips barely moving. He held the book near a lantern, his eyes pressed almost to the page. His ill-fitting coat and his battered footwear stood out to her, giving him an odd look in the deepening light. Wails from the crowd split the quiet, and Samantha felt the chill wind through her thin dress.

"It's time, Sam, if you want to join in."

"It frightens me, Andrew." Sure enough, the mourners had begun moving toward the grave. Andrew took her utensils, helped her stand and gave her a small hug.

"It frightens us all, my dear. I'll scrape the trenchers, and you can wash up when you return. We'll have an early start in the morning. Say kinds words to Mrs. Gerrard for me, and I'll say something for Otis at the gravesite before we leave out in the morning."

April 6, 1792

I shall never Know another day as Miserable as this. The entire Caravan was Solemn this morning as we left one of our own behind. It was as if the birds and insects knew we mourned and joined in our sorrow. Andrew said his words of Condolence and those of us who wished each placed a rock on the Mound of earth, and it was quite nicely covered at the end. Poor Retta G. was beside herself, and I think she would've collapsed if not for several of the men supporting her at the end. One of the settlers took her Children into their wagon to give R. time to grieve. J. sits apart from the Others.

*****

At last they came to Harrodsburg. It had been designated the title of the Kentucky Federal Court jurisdiction, so several of the men immediately strode to the court building, which looked not at all impressive to Samantha Prescott, just another log cabin. Nevertheless, it was civilization, and she rejoiced to see it. The wagons had now grown to over thirty, and some would choose to stay behind until their affairs were settled and surveys made of their claims. As for Andrew and her, and Josiah, of course, they would stay only a few days before venturing on to their destination.

It was a cheerful group of women who toured the fort and shopped in the few merchants' shops. Sammie felt a small amount of remembered youthfulness, and she walked arm in arm with Tilda, as if she were at home with her sisters Marguerite and Charlotte and on an excursion into town.

"Tilda, my dear, 'tis a fine day for shopping, do you think?" She giggled with the silliness of it, as they were surrounded by log structures in the middle of the wilderness; and certainly there was little true shopping to be had and nowhere to carry any goods they might purchase, in any case.

"Oh, yes," Tilda responded, placing her hand to her mouth and giving a mock yawn. "Perhaps an iced sugar will be just the thing to add interest to our day. Ah, for the flavor of strawberry on my tongue."

Sammie giggled again, and she jabbed her elbow into Tilda's side, causing her friend to laugh with her. Sammie was pleased to find a baker's shop, for she dearly loved the tiny iced cakes on hand. She bought several with the money Andrew gave her to shop, and couldn't stop herself from sharing one with Tilda. Breaking it in two, she handed half to her friend and admired her portion hungrily before sinking her teeth into it. "Oh, this is so good, Tilda. The taste is magnificent. I so miss my mother's good cooking."

"And a soft bed, washtubs that work, and bread fresh from

a real oven." Tilda's eyes sparkled as she bit into her half of the cake, and she moaned with delight, closing her eyes and smiling.

Sammie saw some bonnets and hats and wished for the funds to buy them, but remembering her mother's admonishments against frivolity, she bought a dozen glass jars and crockery pots with lids instead. They would be more practical, and needed when Andrew had the kitchen garden harvested. She listened, fascinated, as the women chattered about the new gadgets, but shook her head when offered the items. She used a part of her money for some bolts of calico cloth and soft flannel. She paid for her items and sighed to see there were only a few coins left in her cloth handbag. She picked up the soft packages, but left the jars for Josiah to carry later.

She gazed around as she went out the gate of the fort, and she coughed at the dust particles in the air. Tilda remained behind to haggle with the shopkeeper over a bolt of muslin cloth, and Sammie walked with Merlene, Mrs. Fitzgerald and Mrs. Collendor. The grass was green, the sky an azure blue, the clouds snowy white, and she saw some black birds flying overhead. She took a deep breath and coughed, for even on such a clear day, the smoke from cooking fires and fireplaces was heavy in the air.

Glancing to the left, she thought she saw Andrew talking to some Indians. They were using hand gestures, and clearly Andrew knew their language. One of them was a lad of perhaps six years; two were young men in the prime of life; and to the side, with a cradle board on her back holding a child, stood a young woman. She seemed to be darting glances at Andrew in curiosity or admiration, Sammie couldn't tell. Mrs. Fitzgerald made some remark that distracted her, and Sammie turned to answer. She glanced back over her shoulder, and Andrew was speaking to the boy, his hands moving rapidly in the language of the western country. She puzzled over the incident but decided it meant nothing. He had lived in Kentucky, her father had told her; perhaps he was asking directions to the next settlement.

She left the other women and took her parcels inside the tent, where the sounds were muffled, and the atmosphere was stifling from the sun's rays on the bald canvas top. She was so sleepy. She took off her shoes and stockings, loosened her gown, sprawled onto the bedding and was soon fast asleep.

She awoke with a jerk as she felt the presence of her husband in the tent. He smiled at her drowsy state. He seemed more relaxed than ordinary and told her several stories of the men at the fort. She told him of her purchases at the store, and he approved.

"I'll see that Josiah collects the jars and things that I've purchased. We'll be saying good-bye to several of our fellow travelers, since we already have our claim established by the deeds and surveys. I fear you'll have no peace, for I've bought chickens, pigs and rabbits from Robert Smith. It may be our last chance at such useful critters. I'll shift some of the things from the cart into the wagon, to make room for the cages and crates. Once we arrive, it'll become part of your chores to care for the small animals. I'll be busy working the colonel's land, as I'm required to return the profits to him, and Josiah hasn't contracted to do other than to drive the wagons and help with the plowing."

He took her hand in his own large, callused one. "Such

delicate hands for work, but I fear our time of leisure is almost over. I estimate, if the weather stays good and the rivers aren't flooded, we'll be home in about three weeks or less."

"Home?"

"Yes, Colonel Livingston's claim isn't far away. Over a few ridges, and one large river crossing, then we'll be there. I've sent letters to your parents and the colonel to let them know we've arrived at Harrodsburg. If you wish to send letters, you'd best write them now so Josiah can take them to the fort for you." He rose and looked down at her for a moment, as though he wished to say more. He left the tent, and she heard his footsteps as he walked away.

She quickly scrambled for her pen and the bottle of India ink, dipped her pen in the inky depths, and began to write.

April 9, 1792

Oh glorious day; he spoke to me. I must not think that he has changed his Character, but for a wonderful, fine moment this afternoon, I felt that we were truly wed. It's a fine day, & I have bought several Necessary items for our future Home. I forgot to buy more pins, but suppose what I have will do for now. My money is gone, & I must not pine for what I cannot have. The iced cake was Delicious & I shall have to share the bounty with the men, but I do not regret this day's Activities.

She set her journal aside and wrote letters to her parents and siblings and wandered out of the tent. Josiah was sitting near the fire, and he rose when she came out, her letters in hand.

"Lassie? Andrew said ya have chores for me in the fort."
He spat a stream of dark liquid on the ground at his feet. He had
a frown on his face. Sammie was close enough that she could
smell liquor on his breath. He must have already visited the fort,
she thought, but didn't say it out loud.

"Yes, if you'd be so kind, I have letters for my folks in
Virginia, and I've left a package at the merchant's shop. Please
be careful, for it contains jars and crockery for the vegetables
from the garden." She handed him the letters.

He glanced at the address and winked. "I'll be careful,
missy. Don't ya fret none."

"I've no money left for the postage," she mourned.

"I'll take care of it. I got some coins left from what Andrew
paid me."

"Oh, but you shouldn't have to pay for my letters."

"'Tis alright. A few pence be all it takes."

"Well, if you think that's sufficient. Thank you, Josiah."

She watched as he marched away toward the fort. She was
now truly alone at the camp and thought to visit with Tilda and
her family, but her practical side won her over, and instead she
gathered the clothing to be washed and took them to the river
bank. It was steep and difficult, but she came back with the
damp clothes in her basket. The basket was so heavy she almost
dropped it a couple of times and lamented that she had sent
Josiah away.

She found a length of cord, tied a line from one tree to
another and spread the clothing across the line she'd made. She
stirred the coals and brought the fire into a small blaze; and
without guilt, she took out another of the small cakes and drank
a cup of honey-sweetened tea. It truly was a beautiful day, she
thought.

*****

It was a relief to finally arrive in Harrodsburg, and the men decided to have one last cerebration before they parted, some to never be seen again and others to settle in the valley as neighbors, although distant. The residents of the fort, of course, were invited to attend, and they all gathered outside the walls.

The wagons that were going on were lined on one side of the fort, and the ones stopping were lined on the other. Isaac Shaw would be leading the former group which consisted of over twenty wagons, carts and the Collendor carriage. The horses, mules, cattle, sheep and other large animals had been separated and some sold. Andrew bought some chickens, two pigs and six rabbits from Robert Smith. From Ralph Mueller, he bought a milk cow, and from Verdia Skaggs, simply because she was a widow and needed the money, he bought a horse.

He told Sammie later that Verdia Skaggs had been wealthy at one time, but when her husband was killed in the late war, she was reduced to poverty. She had only the property she had won in the government lottery along the Big Barren River to provide her with a future. She had persuaded her niece Gwen and her husband Elwyn Tarpley to come into the wilderness and claim the land. She was a petite, jolly woman of excellent health, and admired by all for her courage. Sammy was pleased to sit with her the night of the celebration, for she gained such insight into the genteel lady's character. She reminded her of her own dear grandmother, who had died when she was five years of age.

The Collendors were there. Angus Fitzgerald, his wife,

Bessie, and their two stalwart boys and three lovely daughters were dressed in their finest clothes. Tilda Creasy, her husband, Abe, her mother Doreen Patrickson, and her grandparents, Augustus and Molly MacGreagor, sat on the grass near Sammie. All would be moving farther into the interior and had become friends on the journey. She would miss them. She looked for Andrew and saw him talking to James and Melissa Palmerton, and experienced a pang of jealousy; but since they were also moving on, she felt relief. When he caught her eyes watching him, he spoke to James, and the three moved to her side.

He first introduced them to Verdia Skaggs, as she was the elder in the party, and turned to Sammie. She felt as though she should rise from her position on the quilt, but instead, Melissa knelt and shared her thin blanket.

"I've so longed to meet you, Sammie. May I call you by your nickname? Andrew has talked so much about his lovely young wife and her family that I feel we should be friends. But, alas, we'll be going on to Tennessee. It's so far from Pennsylvania, and we seem to only have started our journey." She laughed and brought out a thin, paper fan and waved it gently in front of her face, as though to tell a secret. "I've met Colonel Obediah Livingston, you know. He's a fearsome creature. My uncle, Peter Logan, and he were partners at one time in the shipbuilding business in Maryland. When I heard that Andrew was the organizer of this undertaking on behalf of the colonel, I told James that we must become acquainted. It's been a good trip, don't you agree?"

"Yes, it's been pleasant so far. I was frightened at the first river crossing, but found it to be stimulating on the water. Did you not enjoy the ride?" Sammie was trying to be polite, as her mother had taught her, but felt trapped as Andrew and the woman's husband had left them. She was surprised to hear Mrs. Skaggs speak up.

"I know that old trickster, Obediah Livingston. He and my late husband rode together with General Washington's troops. This is news to me. Did you say, Samantha, that your husband has a commission from Livingston for the settlement of his warranty land?"

"Yes, ma'am, that's why we've come. I don't know the details, for I'm a female, of course, but I do believe there are one thousand acres of land to be cleared, and Andrew has the commission from the colonel." She sighed. "It's such a responsibility."

The elderly lady placed her hand over Sammie's hand. "It will be done, my dear, don't fear. My own nephew, Tarpley, has undertaken the commission of clearing my land along the Big Barren. I've placed my confidence in him. Tell me, Mrs. Palmerton, have you been to the city on the Hudson? I was once there. It's a dismal swamp; the mosquitoes were numerous, and the summer months unendurable."

As the two ladies began to speak of things that Sammie didn't know, she lost interest and tried her best to keep up a part of the conversation.

Those who'd brought along musical instruments took them out and formed a band. They played some Irish ballads, and Melissa Palmerton rose gracefully and moved on to stand beside some ladies of her acquaintance. Sammie felt she could also move on and joined Tilda and her grandmother, who were sitting alone near their wagon.

Suddenly the band struck a loud note and to the surprise of everyone, some of the young Scotsmen among the settlers began to dance with vigor and enthusiasm. Sammie felt the throb of the makeshift drum and the lilting rhythm of the fiddle. Her heart rose within her, something bubbling forth, and she knew she must let it out.

"Andrew, would you please dance with me?" Sammie grasped his arm with both her hands and tugged him toward the flattened area where the dancing was making the grass even flatter. James and Melissa Palmerton were standing on the side of the jovial party, clapping and cheering them on.

"Nay, you cannot think—" Andrew paled, and he looked to Palmerton for rescue. Instead, the man laughed and pushed Andrew forward, and with Sammie's momentum, they were soon in the clearing, stomping their feet and laughing together.

Sammie felt she could fly; she was so happy. He was in her arms, and in public. They swayed and moved to the music, Sammie with her hand on Andrew's arm, and her heart swelled with pleasure. She even liked his smell, the dusky aroma of fading tobacco and horseflesh, the smells carried by her father when he returned to the house from a day in the stables. She looked into his face, intending to tell him how she felt, only to find his eyes looking off towards the clapping and foot-stomping throng egging the musicians to play faster and harder to tire out the struggling dancers. Laughter ensued from the boundaries of the dance, but there was none on her husband's face.

The song ended, and Andrew came to an abrupt stop, releasing her and brushing his clothing to smooth imaginary rumpled creases. He cleared his throat, and murmured, "Satisfied?" He never looked at her. A pain rose in Samantha's breast, and she felt the night darken around her. Andrew turned without another word and walked the ten feet to his friends, waving an arm and calling out warmly to them.

Sammie stood beside a tall, burly Scotsman and his partner, her eyes on Andrew as he approached the distant group. She lifted a hand to her chest, her fingers spread wide, and took a deep breath to calm her thoughts. She considered that if she were tired, perhaps Andrew was also. It had been rather a strenuous rousing of their spirits.

"Ah, my dear, you carried yourself quite well out there. May I request lessons someday?"

"Lessons?" Sammie turned, caught off guard by the question. Augustus MacGreagor stood at her side, and he had a smile on his face.

"I'm sure that husband of yours must appreciate your energy. I would like to offer you a gift for your fine performance." He smiled as he reached into a pocket. "And, also for giving us the chance to watch your husband kick up his heels for the dance. It was quite a sight. When you first asked him, I was of a mind to wager he'd never agree. See what you can do when you set your mind to it?"

Sammie didn't know how to take his words, and she wasn't sure she was pleased with herself. She felt she had irritated Andrew, and she didn't know why. She noticed Augustus' hand held out to her, and she couldn't help but exclaim at the beautiful shell in his palm.

"For you, miss, from the Azores Islands off the coast of Africa. I spent a week there becalmed by a windless summer. I wish to let you enjoy my little island as much as I was entranced by it while I was there."

"Augustus, it's so beautiful!" She took it gently in her hand, lifting it from his palm with care, and turning it to see the colors sparkle across its surface.

"It's not fragile, my dear." He chuckled. "I must be off. I see Mrs. MacGregar headed this way. I suspect someone on the other side of yon wagon desperately needs to have my attention. My bon vivant, take care and enjoy my gift to you."

"Sammie! Sammie, I must speak with you." Molly MacGregar had a hand in the air, waving a handkerchief to get Sammie's attention above the sound of the music and shuffling of feet in the grass. "You who, my dear!"

Molly was huffing and puffing by the time she reached Sammie, and she placed her hand on Sammie's arm, pausing a moment to fan herself with her kerchief.

"You must see what Augustus gave me." Sammie smiled brightly and held out her shell.

"Quite beautiful, my dear." Molly drew in a deep breath, letting it out only when it seemed she must pass out from lack of air. "I must speak with you privately."

"Why?" A new dance had started. Sammie could see Andrew at Melissa Palmerton's side, and he was laughing with her and clapping his hands joyously to the rhythm of the musicians. The sight made her eyes burn, and she turned back to Molly, saying, "This way; I'm sure we'll be alone if we move aside just a bit." She clasped the shell tightly in her hand for reassurance. "What do you need to speak with me about, ma'am?"

"I noticed that man of yours was cool to you during your dance. I wish to express my opinion that it's shameful for that

Mrs. Palmerton to draw him out in such a public fashion. I'm surprised Mr. Palmerton hasn't chastised her for her forwardness. I felt I must give you warning I intend to speak to her about it." She waved her handkerchief in front of her face.

"Mrs. MacGregar, please, you mustn't. Andrew will be embarrassed by your rebuke."

"Ah, this is true. Very well. I'll say nothing. Come, I must speak with Tilda. She will surely get your thoughts off that man of yours, and you desperately need a distraction, I dare say. Take my arm, and we'll be on our way. I shall tease her by asking her if her husband has danced more rounds than polite society requires."

As it turned out, Tilda found the question to be amusing, and to counter the teasing mien on Molly's face, she wrapped her arm around Abe's and told him, "Man of mine, you must dance once more with me."

He smiled and replied, "No, little lady, you must dance with me," and he swept her into his arms, and they were on the grassy field, twirling in great, wide steps, both laughing at the joy of it all.

Off to the side, old man Snyder sat on a half-barrel. His long beard was white in the flickering light, and his ragged hat shadowed his eyes. His gnarled hand held his walking stick, and he tapped it on the ground in a rhythm that followed, if somewhat loosely, the pattern of the music filling the clearing. As the song came to an end, Tilda and Abe swooped off the green, arm in arm, laughing, and Abe gave his wife a kiss, afterward saying quite loudly, "Come, my wife, it's time to turn in. Tomorrow will come before we are aware the moon has risen and set again."

Mrs. Patrickson stepped away from the group with whom she had been conversing; Sammie raised a hand to get her attention; and she joined them.

Molly said, "I'll let you two ladies converse. It's about time I was asleep, also, and we have an early start in the morning. Unlike that Tilda and her man, I intend to actually sleep." She nodded her head primly and walked away.

"I'll be with you in a moment, Mama." Doreen Patrickson gave Sammie a hug, whispering in her ear, "I shall miss you, Samantha. I fear we'll not meet again. It's been a long trip and your husband has been most congenial and fair in his dealing with the settlers. I'm not certain that Isaac Shaw can do equally as well." Sammie was shocked as she watched Mrs. Patrickson walk away, her skirts swishing and her hat falling to one side in her haste.

She turned to see the other ladies by her side. "I must bid you adieu, also, dear Sammie. You and your husband have been most kind. We will miss you." Bessie Fitzgerald leaned in and gave Sammie a kiss on the cheek, turned and slowly moved towards her wagon, leaning heavily on her cane.

"And, I also, my dear." Laura Collendor was looking at her sister as she spoke. "I fear my sister isn't well; but she's valiant and determined to finish the trip." She turned to Sammie. "I'll not forget you, and your gracious mother and father, and your sisters, of course. It has been a joy to meet such a lovely family. Good-bye. Come, Prissy, it's time for bed. You might give Mrs. Sammie a hug before we go."

The girl ran Sammie's way, and Sammie stooped and pulled the girl close. Before she released her, she slipped a ribbon from her own hair and draped it around the child's neck. She put a hand to her cheek and said, "Be a good girl, and do everything your mother asks of you. Can you do that?"

"Of course. Thank you for the ribbon. I'll wear it every day." Prissy giggled, and she ran to take her mother's outstretched hand.

The field had emptied. Even the musicians were stilled, now packing away their rude instruments for the night. It was quite sad. These people had been Sammie's companions, and dare she say it, friends for some weeks of her life. She couldn't imagine not speaking with them every single day. Yet, a new life was in store for them all. They had their dreams and their families, and she had Andrew. Perhaps this would be his turning point, the moment when he would no longer be preeminently occupied with the duties of the wagon train, and he would relax and turn his attention to her. He must. She didn't think she could stand the loneliness of this place if he failed to draw closer to her.

Sammie was distracted from her thoughts. She hadn't seen Merlene come to her side, so immersed had she been in her reflections.

"There go two very charming women. I've enjoyed their company so much. The trip wouldn't have been so enjoyable without such friends to share our travail." Merlene Baumgartner stood a while, silent, and watched the activity surrounding them. Sammie saw Andrew approach, and without a word Merlene turned and strode to where her husband was standing with some of the men. He reached out to draw her near his side.

Andrew led Sammie to meet Jess Bond and his family from Maryland. They were to be their near neighbors, and he said they should be introduced. Electra Bond proved to be a friendly, rotund woman with a pleasant face and pink cheeks. Sammie thought the pinkness came from the exercise of the dance, for she had just come from the circling group. Their children were Jacob, Alberta and Jessica, shortened to Jake, Bert and Jessie. They were as near alike as eggs in a basket, although the boy's features were more coarse and masculine.

As they were conversing, Frank and Irma Gentry joined the party. They'd come with their grown daughter Agnes and her husband Jude Harding. They were from Fairfax County in Virginia. The assembly had grown quite large, and Sammie wasn't sure she would be able to remember the names; but she supposed the matter would be resolved in time, for they would all be neighbors.

The group broke up, and Andrew shook the quilt and folded it. Sammie walked with him to their tent. It'd been a pleasant celebration, but she felt sad that her own select crowd wouldn't meet again after the morrow. There was nothing said between the couple, as she moved into the tent and undressed. She put on her flannel nightgown, for a chill was in the air. Andrew remained outside, stirred the coals and sat, brooding. Sammie heard him speak to Josiah about the animals and then walk away. She could hear faintly the squeal of the pigs and a lowing sound from the milk cow. She sat on the bedding and paused, her pen in hand.

April 14, 1792

We have come to the parting with our Friends. I will miss dear T. & her dog, but there will be other friends for the future. After a pleasant Celebration with two violins, a make-shift Drum made of a pot, a fife, & a battered Horn, the music has died & all is quiet. I can hear the sound of our pigs & the soft murmur of men's voices. The wind is still, but there's a chill in the air; & a restless sort of Anticipation for the break-up of the train. Most will be moving further into the Interior with Isaac Shaw, only a dozen or so will remain behind. I have met our new Neighbors tonight, & a lovely elderly lady whom I wish I had met sooner. She spoke of knowing the col., & of New York City & Maryland. She is soft-spoken & a grand lady of Character named Verdia Skaggs. I'm too overwrought to sleep, & anticipate an Endless night, for he is not here.

— 13 —

Sammie knew they had come to the end of their journey, when Andrew called for a halt and walked around the circumference of a large circle and recognized the markings on trees and rocks.

"This is the place." Andrew held a hand-drawn map, and he compared it to the landscape around them, pointing to a tree, then to a rocky outcropping. He called to the other wagons, "This is as far as my family goes. It's been a fine trip, and you have all been industrious traveling companions. I wish you the best of fortune as you locate your own lands."

"Aye, Andrew. Take care there with you and your missus. I'm sure we'll see each other again. You, Josiah, also." Micah Pollard called to them, removing his black cap and waving it. His wife, Tamara, pulled a loose section of her skirt to her face and dabbed her eyes, as she waved also.

"Good-bye, Tamara. I'm the lucky one, finally here. I hope you do well." Sammie returned the waves, watching for a time as they began to move away, stirring a dusty cloud as they snapped their whips and yelled for their beasts to move on ahead. They weren't traveling far, about thirty miles, but it would seem a hundred with no roads or bridges to traverse.

There were only five family groups left besides their own: Jess Bond, Sanford Kendall, Richard and Natalie Foresome, Frank and Irma Gentry, and the Johnston brothers, Joseph and Matthew.

The men stood in a circle of the small clearing as they discussed what to do first. Sammie and the other women and children found a shade tree and stood for a while, talking. Natalie suggested getting some quilts and sitting. It was quickly done, and they watched as the children ran and played in the tall grass. Two dogs made up the assembly, and they ran to and fro with abandon.

"Don't go far, Nathan," Natalie yelled to her older son. "There may be snakes in the grass. Stay where I can watch you." They stopped running abruptly, and with a wave continued to play, shouting to each other. The toddler, Ned, ran back to his mother's skirts, and she bundled him into her lap.

The two grown Kendall brothers rode their horses toward a grove of trees and dismounted, and Sammie saw a cloud of smoke arise from their heads. She gazed at Martha Kendall, but she wasn't attending to the boys; she was gazing toward the horizon, and Sammie wondered what she was thinking.

The Kendall slaves were clustered about twenty-five yards away, silent and appearing motionless while the men talked.

It was a warm, pleasant day, and Sammie took off her bonnet to fan herself. She drew a little aside and started to talk with Irma, while Natalie and the others discussed the best method for preserving root vegetables.

A little distracted, Sammie watched as Eldon Linford, who acted as surveyor for the pioneers, followed Andrew and Josiah, Jess Bond, Sanford Kendall, and the other settlers as they walked away from the wagons. She noticed the other women had stopped talking and were following the men's movements with their eyes. Natalie rose, gathered her three children and returned to her wagon. They climbed inside.

As the men drew farther away, she became concerned, but hid her fears since the other women didn't seem alarmed. She saw the horses and mules twitching at the flies and sighed. She saw some tiny pink flowers in the grass, and stooping near the edge of the quilt, plucked a few. She looked up. The men seemed to be walking the boundary of the colonel's property, waving, pointing and shouting to each other. Andrew held the surveyor's chain as Jess and the others stood aloof. It was very entertaining, she thought, but soon they were out of sight among the trees, and the Johnston brothers and Frank Gentry returned to their wagons. Kendall stood talking to his slaves, while the women folded the quilts and moved to their respective wagons, their children following closely behind.

When the women and children had gone, Sammie was alone with Josiah. She put her bonnet back on her head and stood near the cart, while Josiah went to the mules. She followed him.

"Josiah, do you think the men will be gone long?"

He had raised the mule's left front leg, and with a short stick in his hand was digging mud from the animal's hoof. He finished and dropped the leg, and turned to her. He gazed to the horizon and squinted, his eyes focused on the activity in the distance.

"Canna say, missy. Might come back soon, might take hours." He walked to the back of the mule and examined the back hoof.

"Should I build a fire and start dinner?"

"I wouldn't, girl. Be a waste of time, most likely." He stepped to the other side of the mule and picked up the right back hoof.

"But, aren't you hungry?"

"I can make do for a few hours yet." He put the leg down and went to the final leg, and raised it against his thigh. Slightly distracted, he said, "I could use some water." He looked again to the distance, but the surveying crew had disappeared. Kendal was still talking to his slaves. One of them had started a fire. "Seems like Kendall done decided to set up camp. Not a good place for it. No source of water nearby." He shrugged and started to the wagon. Lifting the wagon cover, he took the dipper from the peg. He lifted the lid of the water barrel and thrust the dipper into the tepid water to bring out a cup full of the liquid. He handed it to her.

Sammie drank deeply of the water and handed the dipper back to Josiah. He pulled enough for himself and took a long drink, threw some on the ground. He then put the dipper on the peg, placed the lid securely on the barrel and lowered the cover. Sammie walked away and stood under a tree, watching the dark-skinned man working at his campfire. The other men were clustered under a tree, and Kendall wasn't with them. The sun was hot on her back, but a cool breeze arose and blew through the leaves of the nearby tree.

"Josiah, would you please get out a quilt so I can sit on the ground?" He complied and spread it out under the tree. She sank gratefully onto it and took off her bonnet to wave it in front of her face to cool herself. A fly buzzed her ear, and she brushed it away.

Josiah sat by the wagon wheel, took out his small knife and began to whittle on the stick he'd used to take the mud from the mule's hooves.

After a couple of hours, the men returned and stood for some time, talking. Andrew shook hands, and they separated, Linford and the others to survey their own boundaries, riding away toward the north. Sammie waved good-bye and watched as they disappeared among the forest growth. Natalie seemed to be a pleasant woman and a good mother. She would miss her laughter and pleasant counsel. The flowers were wilting in her hand, and she threw them on the ground. She watched a honey bee taking nectar from a large yellow flower and sighed.

The silence seemed oppressive to Sammie, sitting under the shade tree. With no wagons or people milling about, there were only Andrew and Josiah as far as her eyes could see. She watched a bird circle on the thermal, than another, and another.

"Look, Andrew, why are the birds circling?"

He looked up and across to the horizon where clouds seemed to be building in the west. "Maybe a dead animal on the ground. I wouldn't worry, probably miles away. More concerning is that cloud; may have rain before midnight. Josiah, we should get the camp set up before it gets here."

But, he didn't move. He continued to follow the marks on his new surveyor's map. He began to explain. "Jess Bond and his wife Electra, and their three children, will be on the north of the colonel's claim; and Sanford Kendall on the south; with Frank and Irma Gentry on the other side of the Kendall home.

Not too far by wagon, but still they are our neighbors. I paid Linford a small stipend to return and survey my own acres. My land, according to his estimate, backs up on the north with Jess Bond; and across the future road will be the colonel's land. To the south, no one has yet claimed the land adjacent to my own. Linford has approved the spot for the colonel's cabin. He'll draw maps, and the owners each will have a water source, timber and good drainage. The land is thick with forest, and it'll take months to clear the space for their cabins and barns, I suppose."

He took his hat from his head, wiped his forehead with a kerchief and returned it to his pocket. "Josiah, I'm not so sure that I approve of slavery, but that's the way of this world." His voice droned on as he and Josiah discussed the setting up of the camp and whether it would rain, leaving Sammie standing by the cart.

As they talked, Sammie let her own thoughts ramble to other things. She'd met the Kendalls only briefly during the trip, but she found Irma Gentry most congenial. She was happy they would be neighbors, although separated by several miles when a road was built through the area. She didn't know Jess Bond's wife well, having met her briefly at the last night's celebration.

*****

Andrew chose a small clearing beside a fast-flowing run for his own home, and Josiah and he set up a more permanent campsite on a ridge overlooking the colonel's land. High on the hill, Sammie could see through the darkening mist for miles to the horizon. The mountains and forest seemed to stretch endlessly into the distance, with a dense fog covering the land like a blanket. Across the line of ridges was where Andrew and Josiah would build the colonel's home and barn, so they would be neighbors, close enough if danger arose, but far enough not to be disturbed by quarrels.

The storm cloud lifted, and the sky flamed with the colors of the rainbow. Maroon, red, orange, gold and silver lined the last of the clouds, as the sun dipped beyond the trees. The circling birds disappeared, and the wind became calm. They sat near the fire that first night, alone for the first time since they had started this adventure. They heard a coyote bark in the distance. The air was cool, the moon was in its last quarter and the stars seemed brighter than usual, as Andrew began to speak. Sammie pulled her cloak more tightly around her. The remnants of their meal were still on the grill, and she was reluctant to rise and begin the cleaning up.

"I figure if I win the colonel's land, it will all be joined in the future, so maybe a quarter mile to separate the two places should be sufficient. I have this small creek I've named Rocky Run, for there are boulders all along its path. The larger river will flow through the colonel's land. It's listed on the map as Stoner Creek. It seems to be a tributary of the Big Barron, but I can't tell without a better map. Linford said he was certain it meanders down to the Barron. Next spring, I plan to build a road between the two places, to set the boundary line, but it's too late in the season for now. We need to get the cabins up and the garden planted. Maybe some of the neighbors can help build a wider one from north to south that will connect with the other neighbors. I heard Bond and Kendall say they would work on it when they have the time away from their own cabins."

"That'n sounds like a good plan, sir. It always pays to look to the future, I say. Me, I plan to be long gone when this road is built. It's gettin' too civilized for me." Josiah grinned and spat out his tobacco chunk. He picked up his coffee cup and drained it of its contents. He sat with the cup hanging from a finger and gazed at the fire. "Well, I'm for bed. That sure was a good stew, missy."

He set the cup on the ground near the fire and rose to go to his shelter, made from limbs and branches sawed from the tree trunks they had felled during the afternoon. He and Andrew had taken the canvas cover off the cart and spread it over the limbs to give him some protection from the elements. Andrew and Sammie slept in the tent nearby.

It seemed strange to Sammie as she lay under the canvas tent, long after Andrew had gone to sleep. She could see a faint glow against the cloth with her night vision, and thought it must be the moon. A gentle breeze murmured through the nearby tree leaves and sent a wave of longing through her bones for the days of her childhood. She rolled to her side, so her husband wouldn't awaken as she silently cried for the loss of her home and family. The sights and sounds of the day ran through her mind, and finally, she slept.

*****

Through cash or barter, Andrew had acquired a few animals, enough to start a herd or flock, and set her to taking care of them, while he and Josiah made a crude dugout and log shelter against the elements.

Sammie worked with renewed vigor, setting up her home. The cart was pulled close to the campfire, and the table board set up between two tree stumps. She fashioned a bag to hang across her shoulders to carry the stones collected for a fireplace, and fallen limbs and twigs for the fire. She fed the animals and helped the men when they needed it. Venturing farther and farther from the wagon and cart to find stones, she was struck by the beauty of the forest. It was still and quiet under the trees, and the soft cushion of leaves felt springy under her feet. Josiah made a crude chair of tree limbs and a flat slab of wood, using thin leather strips to tie the limbs together, and she was grateful to be able to sit upright on it. In the same fashion, at night by the light of the lanterns and campfire, he and Andrew made a larger wooden table and several stools.

To fill the time while the men were gone, she often saddled her mare and rode around the perimeter of the meadow; she hung her burlap bag from the saddle and filled it with stones until it was heavy and she had to return to her camp. Soon, a large pile of rocks built a small fence to ward off the chill wind at night around the tent.

After finishing the temporary shelter, the men began to build a split log corral in the clearing for the stock. Besides the new possession of chickens, pigs and milk cow, they had three horses, Sammie's mare called Dinah, the four mules and cattle. It took them a week to fell the logs, cut them in quarters and line them in a row for the fence. Making notches in the ends of the quarter-logs, they stacked them five high, with the ends crisscrossing in a zigzag pattern, as was the popular method in Virginia. It was about fifty yards in circumference, since it would more than likely be temporary. They put the mules and horses inside the corral and fashioned a smaller corral for the cattle. Andrew had brought with them seven heifers and one large, black, short-horned bull from Maryland. Once they had time to build a larger fence, he would let the cattle roam across the pasture; but for now, they must remain penned for safety and convenience.

Feeling that the animals were now secure with Sammie watching over their feed and care while he and Josiah were working on the colonel's property, they set to girding the trees and burning the underbrush. Just out of her vision in a hollow, along the stream that flowed through the property, Andrew set up a temporary camp from which to work. Although she couldn't see them, she could hear a faint sound of hacking and sawing while she fed the pigs.

"It'll take us all summer to gird enough trees to plow a small garden and clear the underbrush. I've talked to Kendall who's our neighbor on the west. He's set his people to chopping enough trees for the cabin and the foundation for a barn. That's about all they'll have time for before cold weather sets in." Andrew was sitting on a stone, his hands held out to the warmth of the fire, talking with Josiah, who was whittling on a small limb. Occasionally, he looked up and responded, but his concentration was on his knife.

Sammie was cooking the evening meal. She swatted at an insect. Her eyes stung from the smoke. Sparks flew into the air when she laid another small limb on the fire. She was careful not to get close enough to catch her skirts on fire. "Do he and his wife have children?" She hadn't seen the Kendall family on the trail, since they'd been traveling several wagons back, and she'd only met them that once at the celebration at Harrodsburg.

Kendall was a thin, brusque man, prone to arrogance, and his wife plump and rosy-cheeked; her hair was dark, streaked with gray, and her eyes a deep brown in color, Sammie had discovered. Martha Kendall had a soft, lilting voice, and Sammie wondered if she sang.

"There be two grown sons, in their twenties, might say; named Clive and Magnus. Clive be the elder, I heard. Keep to themselves; good horsemen, but I donna got a chance to speak with 'em for any length of time." He frowned and glanced at Josiah.

"Kendall says he aims to plant tobacco and hemp on a grand scale; hundreds of acres. Brought the seeds in clay pottery jars; said it's too late to start now, but with the rest of the summer and winter to build his barn and gird the trees, he'll get a good start in the spring."

"Done saw the dark-skinned men yesterday through the treetops; one of the sons with a black bullwhip." Josiah paused in his whittling and spat tobacco juice on the ground. He made a few more cuts on his stick. Andrew gazed at him and then away. "Jess Bond said he done turned down the request to help his neighbors with their cabins. Donna have the time, Jess said."

"Well, it's his business, after all. I want to get started on the colonel's cabin soon as we finish hauling enough logs to the clearing. I noticed the brown mule called Figaro has a limp; you best check that before you turn in for the night; might have thrown a shoe."

"'Twill get that done now; dinner almost done, missy?" Josiah rose and put his knife in its scabbard hanging from his waist belt. He tossed the stick he'd been working on to the ground.

"Almost, a few more minutes, Josiah, if the fire doesn't go out." She smiled at him, and he laughed. He strode toward the corral to see about the mule.

Silence closed down on the camp with him gone. Andrew seemed to be lost in thought. Sammie stirred the stew, and she took a hooked-ended metal rod that Josiah had made for her and pulled the pot off the grill. Using the same rod, she pulled the pumpkin from the coals. She took a heavy cloth, lifted it to the table and let it rest while she made a batter for the hoecakes.

"Andrew, if you have time, will you look at the pigs; I believe we'll have some piglets soon."

Andrew raised his head and squinted at her through the smoke. "What, piglets?"

"Yes." She sliced the pumpkin in half with a sharp knife, being careful to not cut her fingers.

"I'm surprised. Old Smith has given us a bonus; I'd thought it would be a few years before we had ham and bacon." He rose and came to her; watching her fingers at work. "Just out of the fire, that might burn you, if you're not careful."

"I'm not a child." His caution irritated her, although his advice was good. It wouldn't do for an infection to come from a careless burn.

Before she could apologize, he picked up the wooden bucket, and muttering something about fetching water for the cleaning up, walked away.

She watched him and finished the pumpkin; pulled the roasted corn from the coals; and with the meal completed, waited for her menfolk to return to eat it. She had time to think about what Andrew said about the Kendall slaves, but didn't mention it when Andrew returned with the bucket filled with water. Soon, Josiah returned and agreed that the mule needed a new shoe. Sammie placed the food on the table, and each of the men reached for a trencher and filled it high with food. They quickly ate since the daylight was fast disappearing, pulled the horseshoeing tools from the wagon and set to work. When the men were finished, Sammie scrapped one of the trenchers clean, made herself a meal and began to eat alone, imagining her flowered dinnerware nestled safely in sawdust. When their house was built, never again would she eat off wood.

*****

Over the next few weeks, Jess Bond, Frank Gentry and Richard Foresome came to help Andrew; while on different days, Andrew, Josiah and Gentry helped Bond and the others clear their land. With the cooperation among the near neighbors, the larger trees were girded, the smaller ones felled for firewood and fences, and the brush hauled into the center of the clearings to be burned. Each family soon had a shell of a dwelling and could begin their plowing and sowing. There was a constant brownish-red glow against the sky from the brush fires, and the smoke stung their eyes.

The bottomland was greening with the addition of the tobacco seedlings, which were sprouting ever-larger leaves. Gentry remarked on their growth and offered to help harvest the crop in the fall, for a few of the dried leaves in payment. His own stock of tobacco was dwindling, and he had no funds to purchase more.

At times, when the wind was from that direction, from across the forest Sammie could hear the sound of trees felled and axes biting into the brown flesh, shaping the logs for the Kendall slave cabins. For days, smoke poured from in between the treetops, telling of waste from the felled trees being burned. The adjacent residence was too far to be seen, but less than half a day's ride on a horse; and two of those days, the acrid smoke burned the eyes of those working Andrew's claim. Sammie expressed interest in someday visiting Martha Kendall, but Andrew didn't seem favorable, so she dropped her inquiries.

Sammie watched as Andrew and Josiah gathered river rocks and stones to build a solid foundation for the colonel's cabin on the top of a ridge about a quarter of a mile away. Mules were harnessed to the larger stones, and they were dragged from the riverbed up the crest of the ridge. Using home-built hoists, the men lifted the logs one at a time to build the walls. Soon, a one room snug cabin with rock fireplace and three glassless windows, one on each side wall away from the door, was standing in the clearing. It was about twenty feet by thirty-five feet and rectangular in shape, with a small lean to for storage. It was constructed to satisfy the requirements of the agreement with the colonel. Andrew and Josiah made a corral of split logs crisscrossed with timber, similar to the one they had built at his own shelter.

Thus, he was satisfied that he had done what was required by the terms of his agreement with Colonel Livingston, and he sent Josiah off to Harrodsburg for news and to file his papers of ownership, given him by the surveyor. He sent letters to Livingston, his uncle and to her parents letting them know that they'd built the cabin. He didn't tell them that he and Sammie weren't camped directly on the property of Colonel Livingston, but just outside its perimeter, so the property would be his own when he completed the required improvements. He claimed only one hundred sixty acres by Linford's calculations. Josiah was gone over two weeks. And, surprisingly, Sammie missed the old man. She hoped he would bring back much-needed supplies of flour, cornmeal, and whale oil for the lanterns.

While the hired man was gone, Andrew plowed a space to plant summer vegetables on his own property. She helped him plant the seeds; the plot was small at first, but he intended to increase it as he had time to fell more trees and clear the land.

Josiah returned with the news of Kentucky statehood. There had been a large celebration, and he described the fireworks, the horse racing, and the long-winded speeches from the politicians.

"So, you enjoyed your time with the hob-nobbers, heh?" Andrew teased him. "My own family is politically inclined, and they've campaigned vigorously for this moment. It's partially the reason my uncle Livingston sent me to complete his warrant. He wants the family to have a foothold in the new state's lands." He paused a moment. "He'd have come himself if he'd been able. But, he sustained a wound in the war that still troubles him. A shoulder wound."

"Andrew! Father didn't tell me that, only that he was infirm. I'm sorry to hear about your uncle's wound. I wondered why the property was so important to him. And, you agreed to come on his behalf." Sammie stirred the dumplings in her pot, seemingly lost for the moment in her thoughts.

"Tell us more about the horse racing, Josiah," Andrew asked. "That must have been exciting."

"Aye, 'twas. The dust they stirred would choke a frog. Ya shudda heard the cheers when the leaders crossed the line, though I 'pect a good time be had by even those that came in last, from the men crowded 'round to enjoy the smell of victory on the horses' flanks."

"And the drink they must have consumed afterward. My aunt wouldn't have approved." Andrew smirked. His voice took a darker tone as he stepped to the open door and looked out toward the sun-drenched hills in the distance. "She would have written in a clause requiring them to win only if they fell off their horses halfway there."

"Andrew, that's cruel." Sammie hushed him. "You shouldn't say such things."

"If you knew—" He abruptly withdrew from the door, shrugged and clapped Josiah on the shoulder. "Tell me, friend, what's the political bent of our new state's leaders? Are we to have a slave state or free? There was some discussion of it while I was with my uncle in Washington City."

"Oh, Andrew. Do you think it's possible? Father didn't approve of slavery, although he said it's the law of the land, and we must respect those who benefit financially from the practice. He said if only the lawmakers would realize there are poor whites needing the work as well."

"Nay, I think not. I saw dark-skinned drivers in fancy livery drivin' the very carriages in which the new men of power arrived to give their speeches." Josiah nodded sagely. "No man desirin' power to rule over other men 'twill give up any portion of that power, whether to another country, or to the man who brushes his horse and tills his fields."

"I say, Josiah, I believe you should be a politician. You've become a philosopher." Andrew frowned. "Even General Washington and Thomas Jefferson own slaves. It's the world's

141

view." Andrew rapped his knuckles on the tabletop. "I've seen for myself around the wharfs of Baltimore the cruelty in the practice." He seemed to withdraw into himself.

"How sad that is," Sammie was back to her pot, stirring the dumplings; her hair fell in damp tendrils from the heat of the fire. The light of the flames brought a bright glow to her countenance.

"Well, the discussion shall have to wait until another day. Josiah, were you able to achieve the goal of your trip?"

"Aye, sir." The elder man laid a cloth satchel on the table, untied the straps, pulled out several large packets of papers and offered them to Andrew. The papers confirmed that Andrew wasn't camped directly on the property of Colonel Livingston, but just outside its perimeter.

"Are they certain? The land agent accepted the survey?" Andrew was pleased as he compared his own maps to the paperwork returned from the settlement by Josiah. He strode outside the shelter and looked at the improvements they'd completed. "What about the neighbors? Have they filed their papers, yet?"

"Only Jess Bond and Frank Gentry. I asked at the court-house." He shuffled his feet and looked at the ground. "Just out of curiosity, ya understand."

"Now, you wouldn't be thinking of filing on that unclaimed land to the south, would you?"

"No, sir. I can't afford the land. Besides, I be from England, came over in '75. I done heard about the high mountains in the west and the western ocean, and I done took an urge to see 'em."

Sammie watched as his ears grew red from embarrassment.

Andrew drew in a deep breath and let it out, shaking his head. "But, about this tract of land. There's the stone circle," and he pointed to the rocks on the hillside just visible through the trees. "The deed says the boundary goes to the white oak on the hill, adjacent to the colonel's land." He pointed to the south. "And, that way twenty poles to the black walnut, so the survey just proves it." He pointed to the southern edge of the meadow.

"Aye, sir, it's all yours, just as you planned." Josiah had a twinkle in his eyes.

"What's that?" Andrew frowned. "You thought it might already be taken?"

"Such a pretty site? 'Twus bound to be claimed before long." He winked at Sammie. "I got a more recent surveyor's map, one just drawn up," and he pulled a sheaf out of a jacket pocket, "that shows this portion hereabouts is claimed." He pointed to an area that said, Prescott Tract, 320 Acres.

"What's this, man?" Andrew pulled the paper from his hand, flattening it out and tracing the outlines. "This includes both properties. How is that?"

"Made sure the extra land 'twern't registered as government warranty land, and I done added it to your claim. Now you'll have no neighbors to worry ya with their troubles." In clarification, he pointed to a large portion of the survey map with parallel lines drawn on it. "This area up to yours with the lines 'tis Indian owned."

"Josiah, how could we have been so fortunate to have you along? So much land." Sammie clapped her hands, truly joyful. Her rock could stay! She ran to Josiah and threw her arms around his neck and gave him a hug.

"No need for that, lassie. I just did what needed to be done."

"You did well, Josiah. Sammie's correct, we are fortunate to have you along. I suppose we must make improvements to keep this additional property, but that can be done. How much land have I gained title to?" He looked like he couldn't believe his good fortune.

"Three hundred twenty acres, I believe, thereabouts, none of it registered as government warranty land." He grinned at them. "Ya didn't quarrel over me being a Red Coat, sir." There was a gleam in his eyes, familiar to Sammie.

"No. The war's over and done. We won't mention it again."

"Ah, Mr. Prescott." The hired man paused, waiting on Andrew's attention.

"Yes, what is it?" Andrew gazed at the older man. Why the formal title?

"Sir, there be a letter, but I hesitated to show it to ya when ya was so excited and all." He reached out a paper he took from his pocket.

"A letter? But, how would anyone know to send a letter here for me?" He glanced at the paper in his hand, a puzzled frown on his face. He broke the wax seal and spread the paper so he could read. His face blanched and he gave a loud curse at the news.

"What is it? What does it say?" Samantha was alarmed at the look on Andrew's face. He had grown ashen and very still. "Andrew!"

"'Tis bad news, my dear. My cousin, Jemima's son, is dead. The letter is from my uncle Prescott. Apparently, he sent it shortly after we left Virginia, knowing we'd arrive here by summer." He withdrew from her and gazed down at the coals in the fire pit. He unconsciously picked up a stick and stirred the coals until the flame flared up and the sparks flew into the air. He angrily threw the stick into the flames. "They found him in the gutter one night, awash in the filth of the street. When he didn't come home after a visit to his club, Jemima sent a servant to look for him. The local magistrate ruled the death mischief by persons unknown." He grew silent, and Josiah quietly walked to the wagon to give them privacy.

"I'm sorry, Andrew. I never met Jemima's son, but I'm sure he was a fine man. Younger than you, I believe?"

"Yes, just a lad really; only one and twenty. My aunt will sorely miss him. He's my heir; I left a will, in case I didn't return from this expedition into the Interior. My uncle knew the details; that's one of the things I discussed with your father before our wedding." He looked around as though realizing that Josiah had left. He took the papers and put them in his metal box and locked it. He came from the tent, strolled to the wood pile and began to chop firewood. Josiah walked into the forest, and soon, Sammie heard the sound of a saw.

June 7, 1792

Everything about me is quiet as I am alone again. The Weather continues fair, so I cooked a pot of beans. Baking bread is a tedious Chore & I have found making hoe cakes or fried pies work best. I can bake Biscuits fairly well in the top of the Dutch oven, or as dumplings with a chicken or rabbit. I sorely miss the sweet cakes & pies of home. Going through the supplies today, I noticed three jars of vegetables were Spoiled & had to be thrown away. I emptied the jars

& cleaned them thoroughly, for glass & crockery are scarce in the Wilderness that is our home. I saw a deer run out of the forest, & am not sure who was the more frightened; he or I. J. has brought news of Kantuckie statehood. My father will be pleased. Perhaps this is the reason he sent me away; to make his own imprint upon this land; as he has done in his Virg. I fear he'll be Disappointed; as my life is not what I had Hoped it would be. A. seemed pleased, even if I was surprised at his remark about his Cousin's death. Still, there must be a reason for it, even if he keeps it harbored deeply inside. In any case, this is news for Rejoicing. The people of this land will have rights in their Governing, and that is as it should be. At last, the Dreams and aspirations of the W. Virg. people have come into fruition.

— 14 —

During the summer months, two days a week Andrew worked on his own land; four days he worked on Livingston's claim. By fall, he had a cabin and had planted the cleared ground on each claim, with small green seedlings of wheat grown about six inches tall. About two acres on his own land was planted in tobacco for a cash crop to use for their necessary supplies. Josiah, when not felling logs or using a draw knife to remove the bark and small twigs, spent his time making serviceable furniture from the wood. He was a skilled carpenter and woodsman, using the few tools they had brought to the best advantage. Thus, each man had his duties, and worked well together.

On Sunday, Andrew rested from his labors, or went hunting for wild game along the streams that flowed through both properties. Occasionally, he went to help his neighbors and came back with news of the area. From time to time, the neighbors congregated at one farm or another for religious services or a harvest feast. Rarely did the Kendall family join them. Andrew reported that the Kendall slaves had finished the large barn required to dry the tobacco leaves being grown on Kendall's property.

As the days grew shorter, and the wind blew briskly from the north, the men spent more time on the Prescott claim. Slowly, using the temporary dugout and log shelter as a beginning, they built high walls around it and fashioned a fireplace with the stones that Sammie had collected during the summer.

This cabin was smaller than the colonel's, about twelve feet by twenty feet, with the fireplace at one end and two doors. A window was on the opposite wall and another near the front door. It was only a shell and had a dirt floor, but Andrew had plans to build a wooden floor during the long winter months when the outside work would be limited. There was a single flat stone step leading to the outside door. A large pile of logs was stacked along the northern outside wall that Josiah would fashion into timber to be used for the flooring, and chopped shorter kindling for the fireplace.

As soon as Andrew had the shelter outfitted with oiled cloth for windows and crude doors, he plowed a space to plant fall vegetables. Sammie helped him plant the seeds, working at Andrew's side.

As the weather grew cooler, Sammie made a paste of flour and water and glued the cloth from the rest of her petticoats to the inside walls and pasted the many sheets of newspapers they had acquired over another wall, until all the paper was gone, and provided a rude insolation from the harsh wind. The pages grew yellowed and stained from smoke and cooking grease but some of the print was still visible, and it kept out the howling wind.

When Josiah tore the cloth of his trousers, she used the shears and cut off the two legs, sewed the parts together and stuffed it with chicken feathers for a pillow. He laughed but wore the top part of the trousers when inside the house, to save his other pairs.

The winter was harsh and long. One night, there was a sprinkle of snow on the ground and ice hung from the tree branches, when a howling wolf in the distance woke Sammie in the night. Unsettled, she arose, pulled aside the blanket that separated the bed and stepped into the great room that made up the rest of the cabin. Lighting a lamp, she seated herself in a chair and pulled her sewing into her lap. The howling came again, closer than before, and she shivered. Unlatching the wooden shutter, she peered out the window and marveled at the white ground. The moon was bright enough that she could see the corral and the cattle milling about nervously. Finding nothing untoward, she settled back into her chair and picked up her sewing, adding a few stitches before deciding the room had grown too cold to continue without adding more wood to the fading fire. The coals leaped in bright sparks as she dropped on two small wedges of wood. They soon crackled with warmth, and she pulled her chair closer to the flames, pleased with the added light to help her with her sewing.

She jumped when she heard the sound of a log or something falling outside the cabin.

"I cannot sew with that ruckus outdoors," she muttered. She moved to the mantle and reached for one of the two weapons. She dared not use Andrew's new one, as he treasured it too highly for her to touch. The other had a barrel as long as she was tall. The scored metal gleamed, as Andrew took great care of his tools, but the battered stock showed the use it had received in hard situations. It was a musket, for which she'd need to add powder and insert the ball down the barrel, but Josiah had taught her how to use it, and she had no qualms about doing so.

Pulling on her heavy coat, she worked her arms in the sleeves and buttoned it securely. With a cautious glance, she opened the door, leaning the gun out, and drew back in, breathing heavily. Wolves! Creeping around the corral! Two, she thought, wanting what wasn't theirs to take. She thought of Andrew's work to acquire enough livestock to enable them to live successfully through the winter. If they began losing their animals to these wolves, she was certain the predators would see their farm as an easy food source and return again and again. It was up to her to convince them otherwise.

She laughed at herself, realizing she hadn't loaded the gun. What good was that to her? The coat, too, was a hindrance, and she slipped it off; and with movements practiced at Josiah's side, she soon had the gun primed and ready to fire. She stepped outside, shivering in the cold, braver now, knowing she was protecting what was hers. She moved quietly towards the corral, the white of the snowfall revealing the wolves' prints as they had circled the corral. One set led inside the corral through a narrow opening at the side of the gate. She searched, finding one wolf sneaking up on the bull; the other was near the shed where the milk cow was tethered.

"That does it," she said, pulling the gun to ready. "I might not mind sparing one of the cows, or even the bull, but I will not let you get my milk cow." More determined than ever, she boldly strode a few yards from the wolf, lifted her weapon to her shoulder, aimed and pulled the trigger. The powder in the chamber exploded, sending the gun into her shoulder with a mighty kick, and her body twisted sideways, throwing her off balance, causing her to stumble and fall to the ground. The wolf yelped and lay still. The second animal moved her direction, its body low to the ground, and it paused at the fence, before working its way underneath and directly toward her.

"No, you don't!" She had no time to reload the weapon, and she'd brought no additional bullets outside, but that didn't mean she was weaponless. She reached for the nearest dried cow chip, still covered with a light coating of snow, and threw it at the animal. She quickly rolled away and rose to her feet. The wolf stopped, as if startled. She threw another, then another, finally yelling, "Go away, you evil creature. There's nothing here for you. Go! Scat!"

The animal began to growl, and in desperation, she spied a rock. She threw it with all her strength, hitting the wolf in the side. It yelped and began to back away. By then, the barnyard animals had become restless, stomping their hooves, pawing the ground and creating great clouds of steam from their nostrils as they snorted their fear.

Sammie became emboldened, and she ran toward the wolf, picking up sticks and stones or cow chips and throwing them at it. The animal began to slink away but looked back at her, and frustrated, she ran straight toward the creature, relieved to see it scamper away, its tail tucked between its legs.

Relieved, she picked up the heavy musket, holding it more as a club than a true weapon. It reassured her to have her hand around it. She cautiously poked the dead wolf in the side, relieved he didn't stir. The cattle had moved to the far side of the corral, and mooing noises filled the night. She made her way back to the cabin and stepped inside; and beginning to shake with delayed fear, she felt tears running down her cheeks. She took a knife from its place on the wall, sat in her chair, pulled her sewing to her lap, but didn't begin to work on it. Instead, she gazed into the flames until her eyes grew heavy and made her way to her bed, making sure the cabin door was bolted firmly behind her.

The next morning she was awakened by the sound of Josiah's voice. She opened her eyes to find the sun was up, and no one had roused her. She knew they'd found her wolf. She smiled, certain Andrew would be surprised to learn she was quickly becoming a frontier woman who was quite capable of taking care of herself in whatever situation was presented to her.

December 11, 1792

It has been a month since I have felt the need to pick up my Pen but I must record the bold attack of the Wolves yesterday. They crept up on the farm while a light showing of Snow was on the ground. I was frightened & shaking as I was forced to use the musket to fend them off. One got away, but J. says he can take the skin of the other for the Bounty to the fort next time he travels from home for supplies. It's a Beautiful blend of gray, white & black fur, & green eyes, but was not so pretty when he tried to destroy my only source of milk &

butter. J. says he'll get a high price for it. A. is still working although the cold seeps into the bones & steels a person's strength. He has cut blocks of ice to store in straw to pre. Our cured hams and eggs in the heat of the coming Summer.

*****

Josiah lived in the cabin on Livingston's claim, and Andrew slept in the cabin with her, so he could claim the land as his own. Occasionally, when the weather permitted, one of the other settlers came for a visit, but they were mostly alone with the chores and the animals. They hardly spoke, but read and re-read their meager supply of books. Sometimes, they would hear the sound of a musket shot, and Andrew would become alarmed, but when no response was made, he said it must have been a settler out hunting for game. Their wedding anniversary came and went with barely a notice, so accustomed had they become to the work and the silence between them.

She spent the long hours working on a quilt to pass the time when she was alone. One evening, she pulled aside the wooden crate that held her prized plates, bowls, and saucers, along with two silver spoons, cherished because they'd been her grand-mother's. Working the lid open, she fished in the sawdust until a cup showed itself. She held it to the light, running her finger-tips over the pattern of flowers, the blooms just felt underneath the surface glaze. Her thoughts ran back to her parents' home, so fine, with exquisite furnishings, and for a moment, she was melancholy. However, she brushed it off, knowing that door was closed, and she reached back into the box, determined to

153

dine on real china once again. She was dismayed to discover a chip on the rim of one of the cups, but there was nothing to be done for it. If she turned it to the back, it would barely be noticeable. When she realized there was no place to properly store her dishes, she sighed and returned them to their sawdust nest until Andrew could build her a shelf where they would be safe. It was Josiah who offered to turn the packing crate into a small shelf to attach to the wall, putting the beautiful dishes out for regular use. There was no notice of the holiday season or the coming of a new year, except that they had completed a fifth of their commission to settle the colonel's land. To mark the occasion, Andrew drew an "x" on the fireplace with a piece of charcoal.

Sammie hadn't touched her watercolors in months; she simply hadn't the time or the effort. One day, she thought she'd try to paint a picture and found the paints were ruined. They must've been soaked in the rain while on the trail. Slow, bitter tears ran down her cheeks, and she finally accepted that her past life was over and she'd never see her family again.

At last there were signs of spring: the ice melted, the grass sent forth green shoots and the wheat was ready for harvest. It was agreed that as soon as they had harvested the early spring crops and sown the seeds for the two gardens, Josiah would leave to stake out his own claim. They watched him go with a deep sadness, for he was a hard and faithful worker.

From her spot high on the ridge, Sammie could now see a large cleared area surrounding the small cabin that belonged to the colonel. She couldn't and wouldn't be so bold as to think that someday it might be her own; five years was a long time, and anything could happen during that time. For now, she was

154

pleased to have her garden patch, her animals and her baking chores.

A few days after Josiah left, as she was changing the bedding, she heard the crinkle of paper. It was from Josiah. Enclosed in the paper was a dried wild rose.

"For missy, with my love. For the nights when the clouds roll by and you be alone."

"Oh, my God!" She exclaimed out loud. "What has he done? The only person in the whole world who truly loves me, and he's gone. Gone forever." She wailed until her eyes were red and puffy and her stomach tied in knots. More than her father, for he'd sent her away. More than her mother who hadn't even written to her. More than her husband, who treated her like a saloon woman, did Josiah love her. She calmed herself and cried out loud in the stillness, "For a whole year and more, he was by my side, and I never knew how much he cared and supported me. But, I must forget him. I must treasure his little gesture for the friendly token it is, and never think of his love." She rose and threw the note and the flower into the flames, and watched until they were ashes.

March 23, 1793

We have said our adieus to our dear friend, Josiah Ferguson. He is for the Western ocean. I shall miss his Wise council & strong courage & Peaceful manner. Through the bad times & good, he has remained loyal & True. He came to this country as our Enemy & leaves us with only fond memories. The sun is high in the Heavens & A. labors on in the new vineyards he has planted on the col.'s property. He said in a year or two we can have our own wine. I dropped the skillet & the corn fritters were ruined.

— 15 —

Their times together, without the presence of the taciturn Josiah, became more and more formal. Politeness reigned, but the times of enforced civility wore on Sammie's nerves, pulling all thoughts of joy from her days.

Summer was long and dry, and Andrew despaired of losing the vineyards. He continued his routine of two days on his land; four on the Livingston claim. More settlers came through on the now beaten-down lane and brought news from the east and the west. A fort was built on the south about fifty miles from them. Andrew decided to visit and trade for some needed supplies. He said he would inquire about any mail for them. For over a year, they hadn't heard from Washington City or Alexandria, and were hungry for news of the outside world.

He was gone for several weeks, and she kept the musket near her. She worked outside during the day, but crouched in fear at night, her lonely heart longing for the laughter and noise of her home and large family. She stepped out of the cabin one early morning, and a bear was casually rubbing his back against a tree not fifty feet from her door. She rushed to grab the musket, but by the time she returned to the door, he had scampered away into the forest. She sat down, shaking all over and cried; she was so frightened.

*****

It was sometime after the bear sighting that Sammie began to talk aloud to herself, just to hear a human voice. She talked to the cows and the chickens and pigs. She thought of all the songs she had ever heard and tried to recall the words and sounds. She thought of Scripture verses and wished she had a Bible to read. Her days had become routine. She fed the pigs and the chickens and milked the cow. She cooked meals for herself. She began to notice little things: clouds, ants crawling on the dirt, leaves on the trees, and birds flying in the sky. She thought she must go mad if she didn't see someone soon.

On the third week of his absence, she was cooking a pot of venison stew when she heard sounds from outside the house. She crossed the room and snatched the musket from its pegs by the door. She heard footsteps, and the door was thrown wide. At first, all she could think was that she had forgotten to bolt the door when she had come in from the barn.

Standing in front of her were three Indians, their bronze skin shining with either grease or sweat; she didn't know, for her heart was pounding, and her arms felt like lead, as the men spread out in the room. She brought the weapon up to point at the men, but it was taken from her by a strong, burly man with a painted face. She didn't scream, although her whole being was shaking with fear. The first Indian said something to the other two men, one of whom was dipping the stew from the pot onto one of the old trenchers on the table. He grunted in response and started to grab at the food, yelping at the heat.

Sammie watched as another man calmly walked to the pantry and, grabbing a sack, started snatching food from the shelves. The man who had grabbed the weapon was rifling through the drawers of the clothing chest.

"Stop!" she said. "You can't have that! We need them for ourselves." She started across the room in a quandary; should she try to run? She started crying, the tears streaming down her face, as she sat at the table across from the uncouth and squalid visitors. A sudden silence came over the room. She cowered on the seat, waiting to be slaughtered by the men. She heard the sound of laughter and looked up. The man who had grabbed the musket was pointing and laughing at her. The other men continued to eat from the wooden plates on the table, using their hands to move the food to their mouths.

Sammie smiled. She couldn't help it. It seemed to come from a deep instinct from within her, born of her loneliness and fear. The men ate until they had their fill, patted their stomachs and burped. Then, taking the bags of coffee, flour, salt, and a cured ham, they left the house. The silence seemed loud as she sat on the floor and cried until she was exhausted. There was hardly any food left in the house, but she was safe and warm. She was afraid to go outside to do the chores. Finally, knowing the cattle and the chickens must be fed, she ventured out, but no one was around, and she was grateful for the milk and eggs.

Four more days Sammie stayed in the house, only leaving when necessary. She kept the meat cleaver nearby and a knife in her pocket, and when she heard a wagon drive into the yard, she was prepared to defend herself or die. She peeked through a crack in the window. She drew a deep sigh of relief; it was Andrew. She ran out the door and into his arms before he could tie the horse to the fence post. Finally, he led her into the house and listened to her as she told him of the Indians and the bear.

"A bear, too?" Andrew frowned. "The men of the village were talking of getting a party together to go after a bear that was seen not far from here." Seeming indifferent, he went back to the wagon to retrieve the newly procured supplies.

Sammie was almost in tears by the time the last crate made it into the house and the horses unhitched. First, her relief at no longer being alone, and now, treats for her to enjoy. The transition from days of shivering in fear to a cornucopia of delights had her giddy. She pulled things out one at a time, oohing over each new one more than the last.

"Andrew, sticks of cinnamon?" Samantha hugged the package to her breast, as if in love. The neatly folded paper was tied with a colorful bow, with an attached tag telling the contents in a spidery print. She reached into the crate for more. "Molasses, flour, and lard. I can prepare anything I want."

"And salt, coffee, tea, hams and sausage, as well as dried beef and venison. You wouldn't have starved, Sammie," he told her sternly. "We have livestock just outside."

"Livestock?" She placed the cinnamon in its brown paper wrapping on the table, lovingly brushing the string that tied it. It hadn't occurred to her until he suggested it that she could've killed the farm animals to sustain her for weeks. She gazed at him with horror in her eyes. "Kill the chickens? The pigs?" She began to laugh. Once started, she couldn't stop. She laughed

160

until he took her in his arms and calmed her fears.

"Come, wife. Sit, and let me show you what these supplies are for. I'll prepare you a repast to relieve the memory of any hunger you might have experienced." He flourished a container marked "tea" and set it down by her package of cinnamon. "Will you let me do that?"

"Yes. Thank you, Andrew. I would love a cup of soothing tea."

She sat silently, while he began a meal of ham, eggs and hoe cakes. She was surprised. She didn't know that he could cook. He spoke to her as his hands slipped wood into the coals to stoke the fire, and organized the food supplies to create his meal.

"The new money of Washington's government has made its way to the settlement. Not only do we have paper dollars in circulation, but dimes and pennies. There are several inside my pouch." He reached into one of the crates and pulled out a leather bag with a flap tied with cord. He rested it in front of her. "Look inside. Even half-pennies. Those are the large brass ones. Go ahead. Don't be afraid to look. They're quite pleasant to hold. I wasn't asked to take any paper money in change, for which I'm grateful."

"Such detail!" Samantha stroked one of the coins, before slipping it back inside the satchel. "I shouldn't wish to carry many, however. They'd be very heavy."

"I think that's the point, so shoppers spend them as quickly as possible. Trust me; the shopkeepers have no trouble taking them from their patrons as quickly as they can." Andrew had half-a-dozen eggs out, and he began to crack them into a skillet. The ham already sizzled to the side. His hoecake mixture rested in a covered bowl. The fragrance of the tea began to encircle the cabin.

"I'm glad General Washington will be president again. He's so popular with the people, Father said. Is Adams the man for vice-president?"

"I believe so. There was talk in the inn where I stayed the night about Hamilton being investigated. He feels we shouldn't be bound to honor our treaty with France, or to repay our country's debts to France in advance. Some feel Napoleon has brought his war upon himself, as Hamilton does, and it's none of our business. The man might very well quit the Cabinet over this matter. I'd not be surprised if he did."

"No, although I have little opinion on the matter. What besides politics did you hear?"

"I spoke with Lucy Cargill." His face brightened, as if teasing, as he scooped the eggs and ham from the skillet. "You might remember, she's the wife of the butcher. She asked about you and wished you well."

"That's kind of her, but I don't really remember meeting her." She poured the tea into a cup and sniffed the sweet aroma. She sat down to drink it.

"I, neither, but she did ask, and I promised her I'd mention it to you. The fort is now complete, with log walls and four tall towers for viewing the countryside. There are more soldiers milling about than I've seen in many a year. I suppose we're as safe as we can be. Kentucky's no longer a wild land of savages and dangerous beasts, not with our militia nearby." He bunched a handful of hoecake batter in one fist, flattened it, and dropped it inside the skillet, pressing it down with his fingers. After only a moment, he flipped it over to brown on the opposite side. The aroma filled the room.

"You tease, surely. I've been a witness of the wild beasts and Indians nearby." Sammie found this small scene of domestic tranquility to be the salve she'd needed. The days of trauma and despair were fading from her thoughts. "Tell me more, of something beautiful. Were the flowers blooming in the fields?"

"Everywhere, white and yellow, and one patch of purple just a mile from here. The strawberries are ripening and cast a red carpet of color among the greenery of the vines. Oh, here." He dusted cornmeal from one hand and pulled three letters from his pocket. He replaced one and laid the other two aside.

"May I read them?" Sammie's eyes devoured the possibilities of the news inside, as if they were already open.

"As you're eating. I wish to read them to you."

Once the meal was laid out, Andrew sat across from Sammie, his spoon in one hand, and the first opened letter in the other. Between bites, he began to read.

Daughter Samantha:

I take my pen in hand to inform you of family matters of which you cannot be aware. Our home life has been busy since you've been away. Little John, your new brother, is now toddling across the floor. I fear every day he will break something, but your father says he is just a child, and I must let him have some freedom. Sally had the measles, and the doctor insisted she be Quarantined. The other children thought it Excellent, as they spent a week with the neighbors and were given no chores to do.

We've received two letters from Matthew, one from Georgia and the second from Fort Nelson in Kentucky. He didn't write much. Perhaps he will find his way in your Direction, and you will meet up with him at some point. I can only hope.

You may remember Jason Neighbors. He has been courting dear Charlotte, but your father refused to allow her to agree to marry him. He feels she is far too young. Marguerite attended the Farrington's formal ball. You will remember Wilhelmina with the Spotted face; she has become betrothed to Amos St. Clair, such a charming man.

There is other news, but this is a large family, and I cannot take more time to write. I wish you the best with your family. I do miss you, even if you do not hear from me often.

Your loving mother,
Martha

Andrew gave her a quizzical glance. "There seems to be an addition to your family."

Sammie smiled, her eyes aglow with surprise. "Yes, another boy. Father will be pleased. I can see Tom roll his eyes. He'll have someone else to tease and play pranks on. He's a very good swordsman, you know, and he and Freddie enjoy the game of chess." She laughed. "And dear Charlotte has a suitor and she, only sixteen. What fun she and Marguerite must have at the balls and soirees!"

164

Her eyes on the other letter, she pushed her emptied cup away from her. "Please, what does the other one say, Andrew?"

Andrew set the letter on the table in front of her, and slit the seal on the second one. His eyes glanced over the contents, he cleared his throat and began to read:

Daughter Samantha:

I have only a few minutes to spare as I have an important court case on the morrow. I do not know if this will reach you at your new place of abode, but I am sending it to Harrodsburg, hoping that it will find its way into your hands.

Your mother has been delivered of another son & I have named him John Nathan Watson, after my father. Your mama and the rest of the household are well.

Your brother Thomas has joined me in the law office and will assist me in this most important case.

I have not heard from your husband's uncle Prescott in Baltimore since the winter. Two letters have been returned, unopened. Everyone sends their love, and I keep you ever in my prayers at night.

Father

Sammie laughed until tears formed in her eyes. "There, wonderful Father, always more interested in his politics and court cases; so he pretends an indifference of family matters. How proud he must be, another son to introduce to his cronies at the club. But, it will be some years, for first he has Freddie and Arthur to entice into the business. Wise Matthew resisted his persuasions and joined the army instead." She sighed. "How I wish I could see them all." She rose, picked up the dishes and began to scrap the remains of their meal into the container to give to the pigs.

Andrew gathered the letters and folded them, an odd expression in his eyes. "I'll leave you to your chores; I need to groom the team before nightfall."

But, Sammie didn't see him leave the room; her mind was on this news from home. It wasn't until she felt the cool wind from the open door and heard the sound of it closing that she knew he was gone.

September 17, 1793

A. has brought mail from home; & political news; Pres. Wash. has issued a Proclamation of Neutrality in the war between France and Grt. Brit; Thos Jefferson has resigned as sec. of State; and yellow fever has decimated 4,000 people in Phila. God rest their souls. Hamilton is large in the news of Wash. City. Here in Kantuckie, the skies are dark & gloomy & A. killed a Deer on the col.'s property. I have spent hours smoking the meat & tomorrow will try my hand at making a deerskin shirt for my Husband. I have a new brother; his name is John Nathan; how happy Mama must be to have another son to present to her friends. And, Charlotte has a suitor; to think, she is younger than I when I married and came into the wilderness that is my home.

*****

The winter months seemed long and dreary as one storm followed another; and Andrew was kept busy hauling dead logs and brush to keep the couple in firewood, until he was exhausted with the effort. One frightful evening, he came in with a burr in his chest. By night, it had become a hacking cough, and Samantha feared it would work its way into his lungs. She bathed his forehead and chest with cold, damp cloths and offered him chicken broth and cold tea, some of which he was able to keep down.

By morning, he coughed nonstop, and she knew it had congested his lungs. He complained of an ache in his throat, telling her he must attend to the colonel's vineyards. Instead, she insisted he remain in the house, and she treated him with a mustard poultice on his chest. After a time he dozed, eventually falling into a fitful sleep during the afternoon. By morning, he was able to dress, and although wobbly on his legs, he ate a bowl of porridge and a portion of ham, and insistent he had to check on the vineyards, made his way out the door.

Sammie went to the hen house and collected the eggs, stopping long enough to calm herself. Andrew wasn't well, and she'd told him so. There was nothing she could have done to change his mind. After returning to the house, she heard a commotion and cautiously looked through a crack in the door. It was Jess Bond riding into the yard, and she stepped onto the porch to greet him.

"Yes, Mr. Bond. What can I do for you today?"

"Is Andrew around? He requested I stop by."

"He's at the vineyards. You might catch him there." She

turned to go in the house, when she heard Bond cry out a hallo. She looked to see Andrew riding into the yard, his face pallid, and breathing hard, as if exhausted. He raised his hand to acknowledge his neighbor's presence.

"Please come inside, Mr. Bond. We would enjoy a conversation with you. I can make tea, if you wish."

"That would be fine, Mrs. Prescott." He swung his leg off his horse and tied it to a post.

Andrew also dismounted, although at a slower pace. She took his hand as he stepped to the porch, refusing to reprimand him in Mr. Bond's presence, but she gave him a stern look. He smiled and said, "I should have followed your advice. I didn't make it to the vineyard before turning around. May I have a cup of your tea, also?"

"If you'll stay home during the afternoon until you're better."

Andrew greeted Bond, who said he'd come to help repair a section of fence, as he and Andrew had discussed earlier. If he was ill, however, perhaps another time would be better. Andrew looked inquiringly at Sammie, assuring her his strength was returning, who agreed, as long as he didn't exert himself and came right home, if he began to cough.

As Sammie was serving the tea, Bond blurted out, as if he couldn't contain the news any longer, "There's been a terrible plague near Cooper's Ridge, and seven people have died, among them five children."

"You don't say," Andrew muttered, taking a sip of his tea.

"Five children?" Samantha was aghast. "Were they of the same family?"

"Three in one," Mr. Bond said, "and two in another, cousins

168

visiting. The children played together. Both parents died, also."

"How did it come about?" Andrew noticed Sammie's distress, and he inquired for her sake.

"Cholera, some are saying, from a contaminated well. There was concern it might spread to the town, but no one else has the symptoms. You might watch, and if you begin feeling poorly . . ." He left the implications unvoiced.

"How sad." Samantha was sorry to hear the news, but she wasn't sorry it happened far away, and no one she knew was likely to fall victim to such a horrific disease. Still, she was aware how easily it could have been Andrew, who had been so sick just the day before.

The day was warm, although mud still remained from the rain that had worked its way into Andrew's lungs. As the conversation wound down, Jess remarked again about Andrew's health. Did he feel up to taking advantage of the good weather? The fence could be mended quickly, if Andrew had a mind. The two made their way outside, leaving Sammie to ponder the tragic deaths.

April 23, 1794

It has been some months since I have written in my dear little book. We have experienced a Terrible Winter. A. was ill for several days with the Fever, but was soon able to continue his work. Jess Bond came to tell us of the Tragedy in the settlement. I am so thankful that the Black Death passed us by. It has been a lovely day, to be free to feel the breeze on my face & the sun on my back, away from the burden of the animals & the cooking fire. I rode on Dinah for a time; but A. has warned me not to go beyond sight of the cabin. But, he isn't here to complain, so I put the horse away after giving her a rubdown & a piece of apple, for he has brought back a small barrel of dried fruit.

*****

During the warm summer months, Andrew built another room across the back of their cabin, making the whole about twice the size as originally; there was now a wooden floor, and he used his evening hours to fashion cedar shingles for the roof of the addition, but it rained twice before the roof was finished, and water had to be swept from the flooring. Each unit was connected by a roofed passageway leaving on open porch between where they could store the plow and extra harnesses, water buckets, and a supply of wood without having to brave the elements during inclement weather. A low overhang protected the couple from storms when drawing water from the cistern.

The new room had a loft for storage of extra bedding, empty barrels, and bags of potatoes and onions. A simple ladder gave access to the upper floor. Each time Andrew came from the village with supplies, Sammie pasted more newspapers on the walls until both the rooms were snug and warm and dry.

"It's fine, don't you think?" He seemed proud of what he'd accomplished. Sweat stained his shirt, and he held a heavy planer in his hand. The new door had refused to close, and he'd shaved it repeatedly until it filled the new frame with no snag.

"No one could have done better." Sammie walked through

the space, admiring the logs that spanned the ceiling, dropping to a height she could reach at the outside perimeter. "Will you put spikes in the logs to hang clothes and hats? And, that window in the long wall; is there money for a pane of glass?"

"I've already spoken to Richard Foresome. David Galtby, the merchant at the fort, has one on order. He said it might be a month to six weeks until it arrives. I ordered two more for the front room. He said he'd wait until the wheat harvest and the miller's making it into flour. With the addition of the twenty-five acres I planted this year, we should have an abundant crop, if the locusts and the drought don't kill it." He paused. "Foresome said he'd pick them up for me when they come, since he's located closer to the village. I promised to help him with his hay in exchange."

"Thank you, honey. I appreciate your thoughtfulness. Now, I would like the bed here, near the outside wall, if you don't mind. And, I'll help you bring in the clothes chest and the chairs." She walked to the place where she envisioned the bed. "Just here. Then I can have the morning sun on my face when I wake."

"You might regret that decision, when the sun becomes too hot to bear." He laughed, but she was adamant. The bed was set up exactly where she wanted it, and he didn't complain when the daylight awoke them early in the morning. They now had space in the front room for a large table, and he fashioned more chairs from hickory limbs, with the flat bottom made of white oak. Her quilting frame was set up in the corner underneath one of the windows.

He put a partition to make a small storage space with shelves. The garden vegetables began to ripen, and she stored them in the new cubicle.

Summer dragged on, and he went hunting and brought home a deer. A few weeks later he left again without saying where he was going. She missed him when he was gone but didn't question his disappearance and continued her chores. They had a nice flock of chickens, and she enjoyed the eggs. He cautioned her that they needed to save the chickens in case there were no wild creatures to be found. It would be meat on the table. The vegetable crop was good at both places, and she greedily stored them in the root cellar at their own farm. There was nothing in the claim requirements that you had to eat the crops you grew, only that you grew them.

December 25, 1794

Another Christmas season is upon us & it is useless to Celebrate, since the snow covers the ground by a foot or more, & no one can travel on the roads. We have brought the chickens & rabbits into the house for warmth, but I fear the milk cow, horses & mules will suffer from the Cold. A. has strung a heavy cord from the house door to the barn to keep him from getting lost in the blinding snow storm that continues Unabated. He worries about the col.'s Plantation, since he cannot go to check on it. He thinks the grape vines won't survive, but is Hopeful that there is no Damage to the other plants & trees. I tell him it's pointless to care for something over which we have no Control. He has been very kind & helped me with the animals. They must be fed & have fresh water.

My mind has wandered on this special day to the loved ones in Virg. & A.'s family in Balt. I fancy they are having roast goose, flummery & mince pies. I would dearly love to see the faces of John, Sally & Arthur as they open their presents this day. I have prayed for them all; does Tom continue to labor in the law firm? Dear Freddie, how confined he must feel in the boarding school. I haven't forgotten my dear friend J. Ferguson; is he alive still? Did he chance to see the Ocean & the rugged snow-topped mountains? The wind howls & moans in the loft & I have wrapped myself in an extra blanket for warmth. A. is reading by the fireside, & I shall Submit to him tonight if he comes to me.

— 16 —

Another six months passed, and they had now been there for over three years, almost silent, lonely, and always fearful of Indian trouble. Two more letters arrived to entertain them. Charlotte had married, but not to the fellow who'd courted her last year, and a child was on the way. Matthew was still at Fort Nelson and his enlistment was up soon, but Martha didn't know whether he'd stay in the army. Thomas was a good help in the law firm, and Arthur, now fourteen, was growing out of his trousers, he had become so tall. He promised to be as tall as his father, for although younger, he was already taller than Thomas.

The time seemed to drag for Sammie; she continued with her chores and watched often from under the shade of a tree as Andrew worked on the far ridge. He stayed in the colonel's cabin while he toiled in the fields and vineyard. At night, he was silent when he ate the meals she prepared, and Sammie could tell that he'd lost weight and his countenance remained dark and gloomy.

At their evening meal one night, Sammie spooned a helping of stew into Andrew's bowl, quivering with nervousness as she spilled her news. "A baby is on the way. I'm so excited."

"A baby." His body jerked with reaction. He spooned a helping of the stew into his mouth and chewed, staring into his bowl the entire time. He said nothing else.

"I thought you'd be pleased." Sammie's stomach roiled; her excitement seemed harder to grasp, as if her moment of joy was fading away without recourse.

"I'm not hungry." Andrew set the bowl aside, stood, and strode away without further response, leaving Sammie to cry her tears of regret alone.

As the time passed, she tried in her simple way to cheer him, making his favorite foods and presenting him with a new shirt for his birthday. He smiled and thanked her, but the days flew by in a tense waiting, as though some catastrophe hung over their heads to harm them. Sammie marked each day with fore-boding, as the summer months brought relentless heat both inside and out. Of an evening, they were able to get some relief by sitting under the shade trees in the yard, and he read from one of their books, while her hands remained busy with knitting small garments for the child.

She had few dresses, so she took one and ripped the seams on either side, used the cloth of one of her aprons to extend the width of the cloth and made a type of shift for her larger body. She wore the same dress until Andrew returned with a bolt of cloth. Her ankles began to swell, so she fashioned a pair of moccasins from an old deer skin. She no longer rode the mare into the forest.

September 5, 1795

My body cannot stand so much work; I struggle through the day, my ankles have swollen & my Wardrobe has Shrunk to almost nothing since I have grown so big. A. has said he will go to the village soon for bolts of cloth, but I fear he is most displeased about the child. Oh, why did my father choose this dreadful life for me? I must spend more time in Prayer for guidance. How I wish my dear mother or one of my sisters could be with me during my travail.

*****

In the fall, Andrew and Jess Bond slaughtered a pig, and it was a treat for the ladies to visit while they made sausage and tended the open fire in the pit. The large, black iron kettle was already steaming with boiling water in preparation. Smoke billowed from the burning logs, and Andrew threw more kindling on it and welcomed Jess with a handshake as he descended the wagon. The men stood to the side while discussing which pig to select for the butchering.

"Samantha," Electra Bond called from her wagon, wearing an old calico dress of blue, a tweed cape, a dingy gray apron covering her large bodice, and her bonnet a contrasting stark pink on her fair head. Her children erupted from the wagon like a torrent of ants, disturbed by an errant foot carelessly and absently placed on the soil. Sammie watched in amazement as they circled the yard, racing with the dog, Red. Jake, the only

176

boy, went to the corral to see the colt standing near the fence with its mother, the dog following him, while the girls, Bertie and Jessie, and the twins, Rowena and Roxanne, marched toward the table board set up in the yard under the shade of a huge hemlock and two hickories.

"I hope you had a good journey." Sammie stepped from the low porch, waving a cloth in the air, walking carefully with the encumbrance of the baby protruding before her. The dust from the wagon wheels was a red cloud along the ground, and it seemed to surge after the children as if alive and overjoyed to see such happiness in their yelling and running.

"Very pleasant. Dear, if I can burden you to give me a hand, I've prepared a dessert for our meal later on." She lifted a cloth-covered bowl from at her feet and smiled brightly. "Bread pudding. I used the last of my maple sugar, as Mr. Bond has assured me he'll replenish my supply. It seems the more I use, the happier he is to provide additional supplies. It's the principle of cause and effect." She laughed, pleased with her joke. "I've also convinced Mr. Bond to share some of the children's clothing for your infant. On that matter, there'll be no addition to our current number. We won't have another one, will we, Jess?"

Jess Bond ducked his head and looked away. He and Andrew strolled toward the pig pen, with Jake and the dog following. Jess stopped to tie the dog to a post, and the boy strongly objected, but was reprimanded for his trouble by his father and sent to stay with the ladies. He sat under a tree, his face a picture of anguish.

As the women were setting up the coming meal on the table board, the panicked squeal of a frightened swine cut the air, startling Electra Bond. She nearly dropped a platter of breads. She laughed, setting it down, and grabbed the front of her dress in her fist. Her face was reddened.

"Are you well, Electra?" Sammie had found the death squeal unsettling also. The girls stopped their examination of the flowering shrub at the edge of the cistern, and Jake jumped up and ran to them. His face was marked by tears.

"Quite well, my dear." She took the bowl of bread pudding to the makeshift table, while Sammie carried the pot of stew from the cabin. "Please, you must let me help you transport the food to the table. The pans will be heavy."

The children played in the yard, running with the Bond's dog and constantly getting underfoot as the women set out the last of the victuals. The time between the killing of the beast and the moment when the blood was considered properly drained would be time for the men to feast. Sammie and Mrs. Bond would be obliged to take the larger slabs of meat and carve them into smaller portions for curing in the smokehouse.

Over the meal, Sammie learned that Electra had received a letter from her sister in Alexandria. The children were busy eating, with Bertie and her mother taking equal turns at feeding the twins. The dog could be heard whining under the tree, but he was ignored by all except Jake. Jess filled a wooden trencher and took it the dog, and he fell asleep after he had his share of the stew.

"What news is there from the East?" The meal consisted of beef stew with carrots, potatoes and onions swimming in cream gravy, peas fresh from the garden, mustard greens seasoned with bacon grease, hoecakes, and the bread pudding, topped with a drizzle of molasses. Sammie passed a bowl of roasted corn to Andrew, and she smiled at Electra.

"They wallow in luxury and fine linens," Jess responded, with a teasing chuckle. "My wife wishes she were there with them every night."

"Husband, I do not." Electra's neck blushed pink in a splotchy pattern. She put her hand on Jess's arm, squeezed it, and pushed it away with a small laugh.

"Mama," her eldest daughter, Bertie, asked, "What's fine linens?"

"Underclothing and such things. The ones you wear are fine," she admonished her. She smiled at Sammie. "What news of your family?"

"I've received no news for several weeks." She put a morsel of stew in her mouth.

"Previously, you mentioned an older sibling, Matthew, I believe. Any news of him?" Electra Bond thoughtfully asked, her cloth going to wipe some juice from one of the twins' chins. Sammie could never tell them apart, Rowena and Roxanne, age three. She smiled at the girls.

"I know only that he's with the Army in Kentucky. My brother, Thomas, has finished his education and is working with my father, the major, in the law office as a clerk. The other boys, Arthur and Frederick, were in a local military school when I last received a missive from my mother. Sisters Charlotte and Marguerite are both married and starting their own families. I hope to hear from them soon." With a sigh, the subject was dropped as Jess and Andrew spoke of the harvest.

At the conclusion of the meal, the food items were cleared away to make room for the dressing and curing of the meat. Large sharpened knives appeared, and the children were sent into the house to entertain themselves under the supervision of Bertie. Sammie was certain the twins would soon be fast asleep. After a half-hour, she went into the cabin for the salt bag, and sure enough, all the children were fast asleep except for Jake. He was playing contentedly with the dog.

The large fire in the pit needed constant tending, and the ladies rendered the lard and made sausage stuffed in cleaned gut skin. Some of the pigskin was scraped clean of hair and fried. It was time consuming work, and at last Jess said it was time for his family to be heading home before the darkness struck them on the road. With great messiness, half the meat was separated and wrapped in brown paper for the Bond family, packed in crates, and established in their wagon.

Sammie provided water and lye soap for the washing of hands. With a last hug for Electra and the children, and a nod to Jess, the children were bundled in the back of the wagon and told to keep the dog from the meat. The company was separated, and the Bond family drove out of sight.

Sammie sighed, picked up her bucket and went to milk the cow, while Andrew cleaned the knives and sharpened them. The sun sank slowly on the horizon, and while they were still hot, he chose a few fried pigskins and ate a hearty meal of the leftovers, washed down with fresh warm milk.

October 12, 1795

We have plenty of meat to last the winter, venison, beef & pork. The men slaughtered a pig and we made Sausage & put the meat in the smokehouse to be cured. We have used almost all the salt. It was lovely to have

180

Electra & her brood of children with us for the day. Sometime in the week, I must make soap & straighten the food on the shelves into a more proper Order. I have felt a twang of pain in my legs, but am convinced it's only from standing so long on them. My ankles are horribly Swollen & I see a faint redness on my face from the Sun. A. is working with the horses; he has agreed with Jess Bond to sell the yearling colt; he hopes to get a good price for it, & will take some of the meat to the fort, in exchange for salt & whale oil for the lanterns.

— 17 —

That winter was mild, and Andrew was able to clear another large section of the Livingston property and plant wheat and oats. It meant a lot of hard work but brought a change in diet. He took the wheat to Levi Hamblen's mill built along the river and was able to sell or barter for other necessary goods and supplies. That had been a mixed blessing, returning to the farmer willing to share his oats when they first arrived. Sammie was grateful for it, for she'd come to truly hate the beans, gruel and brown bread that had been their staple for so long. Now, she could make cakes or doughnuts with the added flour and make a sweet flummery with molasses and slotted cream from the milk cow. Andrew didn't like oats, but it was filling and a source of energy and fiber. His own fields he planted in corn and vegetables, potatoes, squash, pumpkins, carrots, beans, peas, parsnips, turnips, onions, peppers and mustard for a touch of spice. One of the mules died, and he dragged it into the forest to bury him there. He spent some time on the bottomland harvesting the last of the tobacco leaves and hanging them in the barn to cure.

*****

In late February, on a quiet morning when the wind was still, and snow lingered in the dark shadows from the storm of the week before, she gave birth, alone, to a boy with tawny hair and red skin. When her husband returned to the house after visiting with their neighbor, Jess Bond, he was surprised at the sound of a baby's cry. He paused for a moment by the bed, then with a heavy sigh, asked what she would name him.

"I think William would be a good name; William Paul. Do you like that? Would you rather we name him Andrew, after yourself?"

"No, William Paul Prescott sounds good. Are you well? Do you need anything?"

"No. I'm fine. Go on about your work."

Andrew stood for a moment longer, then placed his hat on his head, and left the house. He remained working the colonel's property for two days, but she didn't worry for she could stand in the yard and see him afar off. She slept most of the time and rose to attend to the chores and her child. When Andrew returned, she welcomed him with a smile and served his supper as always, silently. In the night, she rose to nurse the boy, and Andrew sat watching, a frown on his face. She placed the boy in the wooden box that she used for a cradle and climbed into bed. She turned her back, thinking he wouldn't speak, but he did.

"As soon as I can, I'll make a cradle for the boy. You'll be needing more flannel cloths for him. I'll go to the village. I'll be gone a couple of weeks, maybe. I'll send Mrs. Gentry to keep you company while I'm gone." And, to her amazement, he took her in his arms and held her gently until she fell asleep.

February 27, 1796

I'm weak & half-asleep but I must write of my terrible travail which has resulted in the birth of a son. The men were across the way on the col.'s property cutting the limbs from a fallen tree lost in the ice storm of the week before & I was quite alone when a sharp pain encircled my whole being. Knowing the time was near, I had no Choice but to collect the shears, some twine & the baby's blankets and flannel cloths I had prepared. The child is a Boy whom I shall name William Paul, if A. has no strong objections. He is red & has a tuft of tawny hair on his head; his voice is weak but his breathing is normal, I think. I have given the last of my Strength to putting more logs on the fire & penning this missive & now I must rest.

As he promised, Irma Gentry came and stayed with her for the next nine days. It was a time of laughter and tears for Sammie, for she wasn't used to a woman's caring and talk of food and clothing. The woman was middle-aged and the mother of six adult children and several grandchildren. For the first time since she left her home, Sammie had companionship and thrived on her words of advice on the caring and feeding of a baby.

Andrew returned with a boy's second-hand clothing and yards of flannel cloth for the baby's nappies. He also brought supplies of flour, salt, oil for the lamps and bees wax for candles. He crawled into the back of the wagon and removed a hand-hewed cradle with carvings of flowers on the highest end; it was accompanied by soft feather bedding and several flannel sheets and a pillow.

"As soon as the news went around that a baby was born, the women of the village sent what they could spare. Maude Adkins sent the cradle; she said she wasn't likely to have more children herself. Fanny McKinley sent the clothes; she has only girls, she said. I'm surprised how much the place has grown, must be near a hundred families come to live in the area. Old Jonathan Snyder died a few weeks ago; and Indians have been seen in the forest. You keep the musket handy as you do your chores. A body never knows if they'll turn hostile."

"In that event, I guess I'll take my leave of you folks. It's a shame to hear about old Snyder; he came with us on the trip; a nice, kindly gentleman, he was." Irma had to dry her eyes on her apron. She stirred the pot of stew on the coals, and Sammie could hear her sniff occasionally as Andrew ducked his head and left the house.

The next morning, he drove Irma home, and Sammie sorely missed her presence in the house. She sorted through the items he'd brought from the village and found inside a pillow case a multitude of scraps of cloth. She pounced on them with glee in her eyes; she could make a quilt for their bed.

June 2, 1796

More settlers pass along the path & I enjoy visiting occasionally with the Women, sharing food tips or listening to news from other parts of the Country. The men have brought news of the election of Gen. Wash. as president of the U. S. But, I must not linger over my pen, as the baby needs constant attention. I am well for the most part, though seemingly always hungry & my back aches with the work of caring for the vegetables in the garden, but I'm glad to see the Sprouts & greenery, promising a full harvest. A. has brought Tragic news that the oldest Johnston boy fell from his horse & has broken his back; they fear he'll never walk again, so handsome & virile, & only married a year. Poor Sallie, his wife, is distraught.

*****

Using what spare time he had, Andrew, Jess Bond and two of Kendall's slaves had widened the path to a space large enough for two wagons to pass each other on the stretch between his farm and the colonel's. It went past the Kendall place and about a mile past Frank Gentry's farm. Frank had expanded it further south for about three miles to the next farm, the Snyder place.

Andrew hitched a mule one day to the cart, and Sammie learned to drive it by going around the cleared field beside their barn until he was satisfied that she could handle the maneuvers well.

On a pleasant day in early June, he mounted his horse and rode beside her as she drove down the road to see Irma Gentry. The road was rough and filled with holes and rocks, but it was passable, even for an inexperienced driver like Sammie. William lay in blankets in a box beside her. Andrew had fashioned a leather strap to keep the box securely on the floor of the cart. A quilt lay on the seat behind her, and on the floor a basket of fried chicken, boiled eggs and some potatoes cooked with bacon pieces. There was a large jug of water for their thirst.

The animals clopped down the road, causing a faint echo as they passed among the tall trees and roadside shrubbery. Andrew stayed well behind but close enough to help her, in case of trouble. His long gun was in a leather holster at his left knee, and he carried a knife in a scabbard underneath his coat. Inside the cart, hidden by the seat, another long gun rested, with extra powder and shot.

Sammie felt a sense of freedom as she guided the mule along the path. She could smell the pine and oak forest; a bird flew overhead, and she watched it soar on the thermal until the mule took her attention back to her business. She passed the vast Kendall plantation and saw the workers in the tobacco and hemp fields, male and female, and she wondered at such industry. She slowed down as she passed their cabin, but she saw no one so continued with her steady pace. She turned her head to see if Andrew was still following. The broad brim of her bonnet hindered her view, but she sensed he was nearby.

About two miles past the Kendall plantation, she came to the clearing that housed the Gentry family. She carefully guided the mule onto the verge of grass and stopped in front of the house. From the cabin burst a cluster of children, Irma's grandchildren, George, Tassy and Philip. Behind them, holding the baby, Sarah, stepped their mother, Abby. Walking more slowly, Irma came to greet her. The talk flowed so fast that no one could decipher one word from another. Andrew tied his horse's reins to a post and stepped down. He came to help Sammie from the wagon and turned to Irma.

"Good day, Mrs. Gentry. You can see I've kept my promise. Is Frank around?"

"Yes, I can see you have. Well, step lively children; let the poor woman get her breath. Abby, go and start the dinner. Andrew, Frank is in the barn; there's a foal coming, and the mare seems to be struggling with the birth. I'm sure he'd welcome some help." She laughed as he took off at a trot toward the barn.

In the meantime, Sammie had turned to the box and gathered William into her arms. She watched as her husband strode away. She smiled at Tassy, who was standing on one foot, her thumb in her mouth, her hair hanging in long braids.

"I'm so glad to see you. Are you well? I've had a pain in my back for a week; guess it's lifting this child of mine." George and Philip moved away, pushing at each other, the mystery guest identified.

"Can I hold the baby, Granny?"

"No, Mrs. Prescott will carry him. Come, we'll go into the house out of the wind." She ushered her granddaughter down the path to the door. "I have a pot of beans on and some fall cabbage in the pot." She stopped talking as Sammie halted in her tracks.

"Oh, Irma, I forgot. Would you have one of the boys lift the basket from the cart? I've brought chicken and boiled eggs."

"George," she yelled at her grandson, and he stopped scuffling with his brother.

"Yes, Granny?"

"Please come and get the basket from the cart." The boy was about seven years old, tall enough to lift the basket and follow sedately after the women and Tassy. Philip came to join him and reached to peek into the basket, but George slapped his hand, and he began to screech.

"Stop that, boy. Where are your manners? Philip, go fetch some water from the creek."

The boy quickly grabbed a bucket from the front porch and headed toward a clear area beside the house.

Irma opened the door to the cabin, and Tassy ran in ahead of her. Irma held the door for Sammie to enter and shut the door gently behind her.

"You can see we haven't much in the shape of furnishings, but please sit in the rocker. I told Frank I'd give up some of my clothing to have the rocking chair in the house, and he kindly made room for it in the wagon. It's my greatest pleasure, to sit in the chair in front of the fire and watch my grandchildren about me at night."

"Oh, but then, you should sit in the chair, Irma."

"No, I insist, you're our guest."

Sammie sat and unwrapped the blanket from William's body. He squirmed in her arms, and she held him on her knee.

"What's the baby's name?" Tassy put out a hand and touched his hand.

"He's William."

"That's a nice name, isn't it, Granny?"

"Yes, it is; a very nice name." She was distracted by George, who had set the basket on the floor and run outside. "That child, always on the run; never has time to sit and be still. Tell me, Sammie, how have you been? You said you've had the backache?"

Tassy grew tired of the women's talk and went to sit in the corner with her doll. Sammie heard her crooning to it. William squirmed and began to whine, so she put him on the floor. She kept a sharp eye on him as she visited with Irma.

Abby came for the food basket and was surprised.

"This is very kind of you, Sammie. We'll have a feast, today."

And, her prediction came true. With her beans, cabbage, corn bread, corn on the cob, and Sammie's chicken, potatoes and boiled eggs, it was a feast fit for a king's table. Andrew and Frank Gentry finished and went back to the barn. The women cleaned the dishes and sat talking, with the children running in and out and the babies asleep on pallets on the floor.

The sunshine lengthened across the floor, and Sammie knew it would soon be time to go. She watched William and the baby Sarah sleep and wished she could stay longer, but before the thought was cold, Andrew came through the door.

"I've hitched the mule, Sam. Say your farewells; it's a long way to the farm."

They all gathered around the cart, and with a final shout of, "Goodbye!" Sammie set the mule into motion. She drove slowly down the road, past the Kendall place and finally into their own yard. She had no time to ponder the visit as Andrew unhitched the mule, unsaddled his mount and took an ax to chop firewood, without a word to her. She put William into his sling on her back and went to milk the cow, collect the eggs and feed the pigs. It was nearly dark when they sat down to eat some bacon and fried eggs. He rose, put his hat on his head and left. "I'll be at the colonel's place for a few days."

The house was silent except for the ticking of the small mantle clock, and Sammie cleaned the kitchen with the tears streaming down her face. When she finished, she went out the door and sat on the stoop, a blanket wrapped tightly across her head and shoulders. The night was warm, and the stars seemed very near. Across on the other ridge, she saw the light gleaming and seemingly as far from her as the moon.

June 19, 1796

It was a lovely day; I drove to the Gentry farm & visited with our neighbors. Abby's daughter is a precious child; with a sweet smile. Irma is such a friend & I so enjoy our rare visits. The night is quiet with a gentle wind; & the stars seem so near as I sit outside to reflect on the occasion. I wonder what M. and C. are doing tonight. And Matt.; is he still in Kantuckie? How tall & strong Tom must be; today is his birthday, three & twenty. I miss them so, but I mustn't fret for it does no good in the end.

*****

One afternoon in late summer, as the shadows fell long across the yard, and William was playing with a couple of bowls and a spoon in the square of dirt that Sammie had made for him to dig in the soil, she thought she smelled smoke. She stood and looked around in all directions but couldn't see a dark cloud, so she sat down and took up her knitting again. Suddenly, she heard a shout. Andrew was coming at a gallop down the lane from the colonel's property. She watched in dismay, scooped up William and waited for him to ride into the yard. Her heart was beating fast, and her stomach churned with fear. The horse was damp from his journey, a flicker of foam at his mouth, and Andrew climbed from the saddle, a look of excitement on his countenance.

"Sammie, go in the house. I'll join you as soon as I take care of Thunder. There's danger in the valley." He took the reins in hand and crossed to the shed where their other stallion, a yearling named Ichabod, was kept beside Sammie's mare, Dinah. She stood a moment, watching, but William was restless, his bowl dropping sand at her feet and his spoon clutched tight in one hand, and she went in the door of the cabin. She put him down, and he ran to his blocks in the corner of the room; he threw down the bowl and spoon and sat. "Mama, come play." He began to wail, and she went to him.

"Be quiet, William. Something's gone wrong, and I must talk to your father. Play quietly with your blocks. See how high you can stack them." She put a comforting hand to his head and drew him near for a short cuddle. "Play quietly, love." She rose, built up the fire in the fireplace, took water from the barrel and filled the coffee pot. He might not want coffee, but it kept her hands busy as she waited. She glanced at William. He was stacking his blocks, his eyes focused on his task.

The coffee on the grill, she poured water into a pan and washed William's hands. He yelled in protest but went back to his blocks when she turned away. She put two potatoes in the hot coals to bake, sliced some ham and began to fry it in a skillet. She had no bread, for there was no oven, but she mixed batter for corn fritters and turned the ham as the steam from her efforts rose about her head. She pulled her skirt hem from a piece of wood that fell from the flames onto the hearth. The door opened, and she heard Andrew come in.

He came to the fireplace and gazed at her, his face somber and his eyes sharp and clear.

"What has happened?"

"Sanford Kendall's barn has burned, and two of his slaves have run away. He and Joseph Johnston and Kendall's sons have gone looking for them. Kendall has let loose his hounds, and they've started towards this place. I saw the smoke from the vineyard. Gentry was with me, and he left to investigate. He came back on his way to the fort to alert the other neighbors. You'll be able to hear the dogs howling soon. I've put the horse in the shed and bolted the door. I won't leave unless pressed; I'll stay with you." He gave her a sharp look, went to the storage area and filled a burlap bag with food supplies. She watched from the fireplace as he filled a jar of water from the barrel and took a knife from her utensil box.

"Do you think the black men will come here for sanctuary?" She turned the ham and went to the table for one of her china plates. The coffee was boiling. Andrew reached for a cloth, lifted it from the flames and put it on the pad used for that purpose. Sammie put the ham on a wooden platter Andrew had shaped just for her use and placed it on the table. She poured some of her prepared batter into the grease, and it sizzled and smoked. There was room for three fritters in the skillet. As she worked, she noticed that Andrew hadn't answered. She looked for him, and he was near the corner, watching William play, but not reaching for him or speaking. She took her wooden spatula and turned the batter so it would be uniform in browning. The pleasant smell of food encircled the room, and Sammie rose for a plate for the fritters. She heard a sound at the door, and Andrew was gone, carrying the bag of food with him. He's left me alone, she thought. Tears stung her eyes.

But, he soon returned without the bag, and she frowned. The food needed her attention, and she put some more batter in the skillet and it began to cook. Her clever mind began to put some facts together. She said nothing, for what was there to say?

Andrew took a cup from the shelf and poured some coffee into it. He sat at the table, silent, and Sammie became tense and nervous; but she finished her cooking, took a cloth and a long-tined fork and pulled the potatoes from the coals and placed them in a bowl, being careful not to burn her hands or let a spark catch her skirt on fire. She glanced at William. He'd fallen asleep on the floor beside his blocks, his soft curls damp from the heat of the room.

When she had the food on the table, they ate silently as was their wont, each wrapped in his or her thoughts. Suddenly, Andrew raised his head. Sammie could hear the barking and howling of dogs. There was the sound of something falling in the shed, and Andrew rose to go to the window. He drew up the wooden shutter and watched as two black men rode his horse out of the shed and sped away across the yard and into the forest to the north of the house. Sammie was alarmed.

"What's happened?" She rose and stood beside him. She tugged on his shirt sleeve. "Andrew, answer me. Are we in danger?" He turned to her with a smile on his face. She questioned him, "Andrew?"

He said nothing, took his long gun from the pegs on the wall and went outside when a group of men came into the yard on horseback. The dogs were yapping and howling and sniffing around the horse shed. Sammie opened the door a crack and watched the men, one of them circling the shed and looking for tracks. She turned back to the room and began to clear the table. She put her large pot filled with water on the hook to heat. She heard the horsemen ride away, and the sound of the dogs faded into the distance. She spread a quilt over her sleeping son and waited for her husband. It was long past sunset, the cabin was neat and tidy, and Sammie was knitting a pair of socks when he came into the room. He said not a word. He put the long gun into its place and took out his pipe, filled it with tobacco and soon smoke encircled his head.

November 28, 1796

I've not written in so long; my supply of India ink is low. I have asked A. if he can bring a new bottle with the supplies from the fort. I tried a few pictures, drawing with charcoal made from the hickory trees that grow in abundance at the edge of the meadow. The wild flowers have been so lovely & Vibrant this year, but charcoal is so Inadequate & paper is at a Premium. I must not waste it although my fingers itch to draw. He said he would bring a bottle & paper if they're available. Today, he took a few barrels of cured tobacco leaves to the fort. He left the barn as I was hanging out the washing. I was filled with pride, for I helped sort the leaves before hanging them in the barn to dry. A. has worked very hard, & the Cash we receive for the sale will Provide new seed stock for the planting of spring crops. He plans to be gone a week, & I'll keep the musket nearby. I killed one of the rabbits for our meal & sent him away with the meat & a bag of hoecakes for his journey. The weather remains cold but dry.

— 18 —

Sammie was up early to tend the baby. With so much to do she decided to go ahead and start breakfast because she was unusually hungry herself. She'd been alone for two days while Andrew worked on the other ridge, preparing a larger shed for the foal they expected soon. She heard a noise in the night and thought that he had arrived, but he didn't come into the cabin. After a time, she had gone back to sleep, exhausted from her labors.

The flames were burning brightly in the fireplace, and the smell of freshly boiled coffee permeated the room, when she heard a knock on the door. Thinking it must be Andrew or one of the neighbors, she lifted the wooden beam that held the door secure.

"Oh, Andrew, I'm so glad you've come. The pigs' trough has ice on it, and the cow hasn't been milked. The coffee's ready and the bacon, too. Would you stay to watch the baby, while I do my chores?"

He just stood in the doorway, looking at her.

"Come in, Andrew, where it's warm." She laughed as she backed away. "Have you finished the shed? I'll get some eggs for your breakfast." She lifted a candle from the mantle and turned to the rude cubicle in which her supplies were kept. It was dark and cool in there. Holding the candle high in one hand, she reached to pick some eggs from the straw in the box and felt the presence of her husband behind her. "How many eggs do you want?"

"None, my lady."

She turned, almost dropping the candle, when he clasped her in his arms. He blew out the candle, and dimly, in that second, gone before she knew the significance of it, she saw that glow in his eyes that she sometimes glimpsed when he wanted her. He put the candle holder on a shelf. She didn't try to struggle, just stood looking at him. She felt his warm presence and smelled the essence that was only Andrew, tobacco, sweat and wood smoke. His face came closer, and she tensed. Her back was pressed hard against the shelves of her supply room.

"You are so lovely," he whispered.

She felt the strength in his shoulders and thighs, the rough surface of his coat, his breath on her face. He was so close she could see the wrinkles on his craggy, rough skin in the dim light from the lantern behind him. He pressed a tender kiss on her lips and lowered the bodice of her dress. The breasts were heavy with milk, and he caressed a nipple and leaned forward to plant a kiss on it. He looked into her eyes, and abruptly he dropped his arms and stepped back.

"I'm sorry, Sam. That should never have happened. Please

forgive me. There's no need for you to tend the animals this morning. I'll take three eggs, if you please." And with a huge sigh, he turned and stomped across the room and out the door.

Sammie was shaking with reaction. She reached again for the eggs, her breath coming in pants. Gathering four; she walked to the table, placed the eggs carefully on it and walked to the baby's crib. She brought her hand to her lips and felt the surface as he had felt it. She ran her hand down the length of her body, down past the now flat belly and to that place that hid the warmth and moisture of her sex. The baby lay sleeping on his back, and she reached to caress his hand. Somehow, she felt the two connected. Did his recent desire come from the birth of the child? With a sigh, she turned back to the table and scratched in her utensil box for the ladle and a spoon.

When Andrew returned to the cabin with the bucket a quarter of the way full of warm milk, Sammie was on her knees before the fireplace, stirring the pot of porridge. She turned with a smile.

"I do so thank you for the milk; Andrew, you must be hungry. Did you say that you'd finished the shed?" She rose and brought the skillet to the table with the hot fried eggs. She calmly ladled three into his plate and one for her. She looked up and saw him straining the milk into a large pottery jar.

"Yes, it's finished." She watched as the pure white milk left the bucket and streamed into the jar. "I think it only a matter of days before the foal is born. I pray it's a filly for breeding purposes. My stallion is worn out and needs to retire to the field. Foresome has a new stallion that we've talked of breeding with your mare, but she's growing too old. This will be her last foal." He finished the milk, poured himself a cup of coffee and sat down to eat.

"Hmmm, that coffee smells good. You always make good coffee, Sammie. I came for the plow. I've decided to get started on the new patch Bond helped me log last month. His wife has another baby, a boy. Six children, that makes them now." He spooned some porridge into his mouth and reached for a slice of bacon. "One of Kendall's male slaves died yesterday."

She made no sound, simply finished her egg and porridge. The baby awoke, and she rose and went to him. When she turned back, Andrew was gone. She heard sounds in the yard and pulled up the wooden shutter from the window. He was lifting the plow into the wagon. She felt the warmth of her child in her arms, and she hugged him close and planted a tiny kiss on his forehead. The sun peeped over the horizon, saw that it was good, and rose in the sky. Later, as she left the cabin to feed the pigs, she thought of the events of the morning, smiled and went on with her chores.

*****

Toward the end of August, Sammie heard a disturbance in the yard. She had collected the eggs, with William at her feet, holding a piece of wood in his hand. She peeked through a hole in the logs of the chicken house and saw to her amazement about twenty soldiers in uniform. Only two were on horses, the rest in a deplorable state of ragged dress, their coats threadbare, with woolen scarves wound around necks and trousers needing repairs; a few wore leather-strapped sandals instead of boots. They stopped walking and stood in clusters under the large oak in the yard. A couple plopped on the grass, uncaring whether they might be called to order for their careless behavior, it seemed to Sammie.

One man, obviously a leader by his uniform, dismounted and strode to the door and knocked. He was tall and lean, and walked with a slight limp. He had a flat-brimmed service hat on his head, and Sammie could see that his trousers were dirty and stained.

"Looks like no one home." He yelled to the other man on horseback.

"Check the sheds and outhouses." He looked around him and across to the clearing on the other ridge. He stood on his feet in the saddle, the better to see to the horizon. He looked larger than the first man, brawny with arms like tree limbs. His face was reddish-brown as though he spent a lot of time in the sun and wind.

Sammie decided she'd best show herself, or they would find her hiding among the chickens. She took William's hand and pulled him behind a post. "Don't make a sound until I tell you. Don't move." She laid the basket of eggs on a shelf while she brought the long gun up to her shoulder. She was trembling with fear; but said in a loud voice.

"I'm here. What do you want?" She held the weapon at her shoulder, pointed at the man on the horse. His head swiveled around at the sound of a feminine voice.

He slowly dismounted, proving himself to be of average height and tending to roundness, with long brown hair showing from underneath his military officer's hat. She kept her weapon aimed at him as he moved. She tried to keep her eyes on the men on the ground, but there were too many, so she concentrated on the man in uniform with the shiny yellow buttons.

"Now, ma'am, we don't intend no harm, just looking for runaway slaves. You can put down that weapon."

"How do I know that's what you want? How do I know you haven't come to take our property from us?"

The officer moved closer, peering intently. He chuckled and turned to his fellow officer who was walking toward him. "Lieutenant, she thinks we came to steal."

"Ma'am, if you'll put down the gun, we'll explain." The other man kept walking and Sammie turned the musket on him and he stopped and raised his hands.

"Hold a minute, Zachary." The blond man held out an arm to his fellow officer. "I believe I know this woman. Samantha?"

Sammie took a quick look at the troopers gazing at her with surprise on their faces. A couple of soldiers sat on the grass. She turned back to the leader.

"If I put this gun down, do you promise not to harm me or my child? Wait! How do you know my name?"

"You don't recognize me, yet?" He grinned and removed his cap. His blond tresses gleamed in the rays of the sun, and she could see the resemblance to her father's face. "I used to toss you in the waterhole when we were children."

"Matthew?" Sammie slowly let the barrel of the musket drop. "Is it truly you?"

"See, Zachary. I told you I knew this woman. She's my sister. We grew up together on my father's holdings in Virginia. You have a child, Samantha? I promise no harm will come to him. Just put the weapon down." He moved closer to her and reached for the long gun. She handed it to him.

The sound of a baby's crying penetrated the air, and she turned, as a small boy came from the chicken house, toddling on fat, unstable legs. Tears were running down his face, and she lifted him into her arms to comfort him.

"Mama."

"Yes, darling. I'm here."

"Well, Lordy, Watson, would you look at that." The captain gazed at the boy in something resembling shock. He laughed. "You have a nephew, Lieutenant."

Matthew was facing Sammie, but watching the men under the shade of the trees. A few had started forward and were whispering among themselves. "Steady, men, we want no trouble here." The men seemed to relax, and a few more sat down under the trees.

Sammie had time to note they looked hungry and thirsty. She felt compassion for them. She held William closer to her breast, and he whimpered but didn't cry out.

"There's water in the cistern by the corner of the cabin. I suppose your men are thirsty." That aroused their attention. A few of the men rose and walked to the rock wall of the cistern and began to pull on the rope to bring water from the depths.

"Did you say you're looking for runaway slaves? I haven't seen anyone today. Why would a slave come here? I have nothing to steal." She heard a sound behind her; one of the men had come close and whispered to William.

"Hello, little man. I'll bet you're as brave as your mama." He tipped his cap to Sammie. "We appreciate the water, ma'am."

William's face was streaked with tears, and he clung to her, cowering from the strange man.

The captain spoke up. "Get back to the other men, soldier." And the trooper went to join his companions in arms.

"We thank you kindly, ma'am, for the water. We've come a long ways. There are two runaways missing from the Kendall plantation. I suppose you know Sanford Kendall?" It was said in the form of a question, and she nodded her head. She started walking to the house.

"We know him. He came with us on the same wagon train from Virginia." She was now level with the two horsemen. She could see the leader had brown eyes. "We heard that two of his slaves had run away. Do you mean they haven't been found?" William pulled on her shirt. "Shh, be still, son. I'm talking to the gentlemen."

Lieutenant Matthew Watson handed Sammie her musket and started toward the cistern, and she watched him, as he said something to the men. The leader in front of her was watching, too. He turned back to her.

"My name's Captain Zachary Blanchard." He tipped his hat, and she could see a thin red vein in one eye, as though he was partial to drink. She could smell the odor of whisky on his breath. "Are you Mrs. Prescott? I was told the men took your husband's horse. Is that correct?'

"Yes, they broke into the horse shed while we were eating. We heard them ride away, at least someone rode away, then Kendall and the other neighbors came with the dogs, and I stayed in the house, while my husband spoke to them. That's all I know, sir." There was a loud boisterous laugh from the men, and she turned her head. Her brother was drinking from the gourd dipper, the water dripping from the sides of his mouth. Could this be the boy with whom she had romped and rode horses as a child? He seemed so virile and striking in appearance. She turned back to Captain Blanchard and shifted

William in her arms. He was becoming heavy, as he leaned his head on her shoulder.

"I don't have much, but I can offer some coffee and venison stew, if you'd like to come into the house. I have to tend to the child."

"Go ahead ma'am, and with your permission, we'll look around a bit." He frowned as he looked at the sheds and corrals. "Where's your husband?"

She turned and pointed to the other ridge. "He's over there. He works the colonel's property four days a week. Look! See? There he is among those green vines. That's the vineyard, and that shed is the winepress. We hope to have wine next year if the rain doesn't drown the vines." She jumped nervously as the captain gave a loud bellow of disbelief.

"Wine? Well, I can't imagine real wine in the wilderness. Heh, Lieutenant, the lady says those are grape vines over there on the hill."

All of the men turned to look at the distant cleared space to the east. They began to shuffle their feet and whisper among themselves. Sammie could make out a few words, among them, wine and grapes. She hoped they didn't think they could take them, as the profit from their sale belonged to the colonel. The lieutenant came towards them, carrying the dipper of water for his leader.

William was pulling on Sammie's dress and crying. "Mama. Mama." He had a look of distress on his face.

Sammie gave one more glance at the men and her husband across on the other hill, and walked to the outhouse. When she came out, she saw several of the men swarming around the sheds, the pig pen and the chicken coops. She watched a moment and went into the house. She thought to bar the door, but decided it wouldn't accomplish anything. The men knew that she was alone on the place. And, she hoped to have a private talk with Matthew. She put the long gun in its place and told William to play with his blocks. He looked at her a moment, and his eyes reddened. When she motioned to him and told him once more, he made a face and tottered to his blocks, sitting heavily, and started to stack the wooden squares Jess Bond had carved for him.

Sammie went to the fireplace, took the brush from the peg on the wall and brushed the dead ashes into a metal bucket. With that done, she stirred the coals to build a fire; once a good flame was growing, she put two medium-sized logs on the fire. She grabbed the coffee pot, dipped some water into it and set it aside. She ground some coffee beans, poured the crushed powder in the pot and set it on the grill that the blacksmith, Whitesides, had made for her campfires. There was a pot of stew simmering, and she stirred the ingredients and hung it lower on the bar to cook faster. She couldn't hope to feed all the men, and her face puckered into a frown. She heard the men gathered in the yard yelling and the horses nickering. They seemed to be making a thorough search for the slaves. She stepped back out to the porch, and taking the piece of heavy metal meant for the purpose, she rang it against the triangle hanging on a strap. It was her emergency signal for Andrew. She wasn't sure this was a pure emergency, but she wanted her husband nearby. The men came from their places of searching, and she saw the leader run toward her.

"What's going on? What are you doing?' His face was red and damp from perspiration. He gazed at her with suspicion.

"I'm calling my husband. See, he heard me." It was true. Andrew looked up at the faint clanging of metal against metal. Sammie and the captain watched as he left what he was doing and mounted his horse without a saddle and started down the path toward them. She stood for a moment longer, the men in clusters watching, and she went into the cabin.

"Mama." William pulled on her skirt.

She took a dipper and filled his small wooden cup with water and gave it to him.

"What do you say, son?"

"Tank oo, mama." He smiled, and she gave him a hug.

She turned when she heard the excited clambering in the yard. She looked through a crack in the door opening at the men gathered around Andrew as he dismounted and took in the situation.

"William, you must be very quiet, while Papa talks to the men. Do you understand?" She smiled to lessen the tension, but she was shaking with reaction and fear herself. "Go to the corner and play." He went and sat on the floor. It was clear he didn't understand, for they seldom had visitors in large numbers.

She went to her supply room and gathered some parched ears of corn, a bowl and a long-handled, wide-mouthed spoon. She put them on the table and went back for a pumpkin, grown in their own garden, and as many potatoes as one hand would carry. She stood at the table, working while she could barely hear the men conversing outside the door. She carefully stripped the kernels from the cobs and let them fall into the bowl. When she had them bare, she set the cobs aside to feed the pigs, and using the large wooden spoon, she crushed the corn particles until they were almost a powder. She took the coffee pot off the flames and set it near the coals so it would stay warm but not boil away.

She checked on William, said a few words of comfort to him, and he played with his bowl and spoon, mimicking her actions. She poured some water into the cornmeal, added some bacon grease left from her breakfast and stirred it into a batter, adding a little salt for taste to make hoecakes. She set it aside while she cut the pumpkin in half, scooped out the seeds into her slop jar with the corn cobs, added a small amount of brown sugar and cinnamon and placed the halves at the edge of the flames.

All seemed quiet outside, and she raced to the door, opened it a crack and looked out. The yard was empty. Cautiously, she opened the door wider; there was no sound; there were no men or horses. "Oh!" she exclaimed. The sound seemed loud in the room, and William looked up from his place in the corner and ran on his short, fat legs to her side. She laid her arm across his shoulder to hold him back and opened the door wider. Everyone was gone. The yard was littered with horse chips, boot prints and damp spots, but there was no sign of the men who had so recently occupied it. She ventured onto the porch and looked to the other ridge; they were there. While she'd been busy with her work, the men had moved onto the colonel's property. Her eyes filled with tears. Why had Matthew not come to speak with her? She shooed William back in, shut the door and dropped the wooden beam to secure it. Suddenly, she remembered she'd left the eggs in the basket.

She opened the door, peered cautiously out and, taking William into her arms, ran to the chicken house and entered. It was chaos; feathers were everywhere; only one rooster and five chickens were left, and the eggs and the basket were gone. She fell against the wall and laughed until her side hurt. She passed the pigpen and counted. One of her pigs was gone, too. She stopped to look at the men across the way, went into the house, bolted the door and sat down and cuddled William in her arms. She smelled something burning and rose to tend her food.

Several hours later, as the sun was sinking behind the forest, she heard a horse and knew it was Andrew. She opened the door and watched as he led his horse to the shed. She shut the door and started putting the food on the table. She had already fed William and put him to bed. There was corn mush and stuffed pumpkin with sugar and spices. There were beans, stew and roasted potatoes, and coffee and milk to drink. She thought she would have to feed the officers, so had cooked more than usual.

Andrew came through the door, dropped the board to lock it, hung his hat on a peg, put his long gun in its place and sat down. Sammie poured a cup of coffee and looked at him closely. She was close to tears, her relief was so great. He picked up his spoon and began to eat.

"Did you talk with my brother?"

"Yes. He was very astute; seemed to know Kendall beats his slaves."

"But, did he say anything about my parents? Oh, I do wish he'd tarried longer, to see if he had news from home."

"Samantha, he wasn't here on a social call; he's an officer in the country's Army. How would it have looked to his men if he'd come in to a sit-down dinner? It appears as though the troopers are underfed. Stop fretting; he did the right thing."

She poured a cup of milk for herself and sat down. She waited for him to speak again. She took her own spoon and filled her plate with beans, a potato, and began to eat. She had to gulp back a hysterical laugh. Finally, her heart beating fast, she couldn't wait longer.

"They took some chickens and a pig, and the eggs." She held the spoon tightly to keep her hand from shaking. She took a sip of milk.

"Yes, I had to do something to appease them. It seems that Kendall reported that the slaves stole my horse and the tracks lead here and away from here. They lost the tracks in the forest. Captain Blanchard said the runaways left the horse about three miles from here tied to a tree near Jess Bond's place. They took one of Jess' horses, and he suspects they've joined with a small band of Indians. Jess said I could pick up my horse at his place whenever I felt ready. I told him to tell Jess I'd come on Sunday for the horse."

"What will Kendall do now?"

He shrugged. "What can he do? The men are gone, and if he leaves to find the Indians, he might lose his other slaves while he's away." He lifted a scoop of pumpkin into his mouth and smiled. "That's good, Sammie. Would you give me a bit of your milk?"

Surprised, she handed him the cup, and he poured some milk into the pumpkin center. He took a spoonful into his mouth and chewed. "The captain said to thank you for the water. And, the chickens and pig."

Sammie gaped at him. They both burst out laughing, and tears gathered in her eyes.

August 28, 1797

There were soldiers here today looking for the runaway slaves. My brother Matt. was among them, but he didn't Tarry to speak with me. I'm disappointed. I've not seen him since he was a Youth. He has grown tall, handsome & courageous. His face somewhat resembles Father but his hair & eyes are like dear Arthur. A. says I must not pine for things beyond my control. They have taken some chickens & a pig. A. will go to Bond's place tomorrow to retrieve his horse stolen by the slaves. He has shown me a new treat; milk in the sweetened pumpkin. It gives off a fragrant aroma & is very tasty. The weather remains warm & he fears that if we have no rain soon, we'll have no corn crop. The vines are loaded with green grapes & he's sure we'll have wine to drink next year.

— 19 —

In all the years it took to fulfill the requirements to possess the land, Sammie only left her home once. She had a need for new clothes for them and for William, and some shoes since he was growing so fast. Andrew made arrangements with Joseph Johnston, one of the neighbors, to stay at the farm and take care of the animals while he took Sammie to the new village called Cooper's Ridge. It would take a week if the weather held fine. He packed enough supplies for their nourishment on the road, extra quilts, the tent and things to barter. He took corn, two hams, some sausage from a pig he slaughtered in the fall, pumpkins, squash and grapes from the vineyard, not yet of good quality for wine, but good enough to eat. He had cages with a few chickens since they had multiplied greatly in their season in the wilderness, and he felt they could spare them. He also had some deer skins and rabbit skins he hoped to sell or barter.

The first night on the trail was quiet, and the stars seemed enormous in the darkness of the quarter moon. Sammie had almost forgotten the stillness of the campfires. There were no others to entertain them with their foolish antics, no women to talk with, no Josiah to help with the work. Andrew had driven the wagon, and she sat proudly beside him. He remained quiet until after a meal of bacon, boiled eggs, fried potatoes with onions, and hoecakes.

He brought the cover from the cart and spread it on the ground for them to place their bedroll. The fire was slowly dying, and he piled extra logs and kindling close by in case it threatened to go out. Sammie washed William's face and hands, wrapped him in warm blankets and put him to sleep early. Andrew was busy with the mules, and she finished scraping the wooden dishes and put them away in the box holding their meager supplies. She sat for a moment, watching the reds, yellows and blues of the fire as the coals glistened. It was mesmerizing in a way. She yawned and glanced at William, his tawny head barely seen from the top of the covers.

Rising and stretching her back, she decided to go to bed. She sat on the quilts and took off her boots, being careful to clean the mud off with a small stick. She crawled into the bedclothes and felt the warmth of her boy beside her. She lay on her back and looked at the stars. She heard a frog at the water's edge calling to his mate, and she turned her head but couldn't see him. The whistle of a night bird was nearby, and then an answer sounded from a few yards away. She heard footsteps and held her breath.

"Sammie, are you asleep?"

"No."

He seemed to pause a moment, then sat beside her. He watched the sparks and the colorful heat of the coals. She could see the reflection on his profile. "It's less than a year until the property will be ours. Do you regret the years and the hard work it's taken to claim it?"

"Sometimes."

"Only sometimes?" He pulled off his boots and placed them near the bedding. He rose and removed his coat, his vest and then his trousers. Sammie's heart began to beat faster. She could see the silhouette of his masculine body and held her breath. He squatted on the ground, lifted the covers and crawled in beside her. She felt the cool air as it penetrated her warmth, and then he lay still.

"It hasn't been as I dreamed it would be. I'd hoped to roam the hills and valleys, searching for wild game and trapping beaver near the streams. It's been only hard work, night and day, never ending and constant. I suppose it'll be worth it in the end, but I wish I could be like Josiah Ferguson, leave all this behind and head for the high mountains and the ocean." He sighed, and took a deep breath. She could feel the rise and fall of the covers. "Well, no need to fret for what cannot be. Goodnight, Sammie."

He turned on his side away from her, and she adjusted the bedding around William and felt alone. "Goodnight," She whispered. She remained awake long after she heard his steady breathing and knew he was asleep. The next thing she knew, she was alone with the boy, and he was whimpering.

"Mama. Mama."

She yawned and sat up to put on her boots. She shook them to make sure a small critter hadn't crawled in during the night. "Yes, sweetie, I know. The sun's coming up. Arise, my darling. We'll be on our way again."

"Where we going?"

"To the fort. I told you."

"I forgot."

She laughed, straightened her clothes and helped him with his clothing. She rolled up the bedding and placed it in the wagon. She looked around but didn't see Andrew. The mules were standing under a cluster of trees, unhitched. She took a stick, raked the coals until she had a nice, blazing flame going and led William to the creek for water.

She had bacon frying, eggs ready to cook, and six warm and fragrant hoecakes ready, when Andrew came striding up the path between the trees.

"Good morning, husband." He looked at her; then at the child, but didn't speak. He had a frown on his face. He went to the mules and gave them some hay from a small bag and hitched them to the wagon. He checked on the supplies in the wagon and came to the fireside. He took a cloth and poured a cup of coffee. He blew on it and took a sip.

"It's looks to be a fine morning." Sammie was determined to get some response from him.

He looked around and smiled. "Yes, I believe so. As soon as we eat, we'll be on our way." She put some bacon and two eggs on his plate and handed him a spoon. Then she served William and herself.

He reached for the hoecakes, spooned some molasses onto them and began to eat. Sammie was pleased with her attempts at cooking again over the open flame. She ate and helped William with his meal. Andrew put his plate down and rose to go to the mules.

She quickly finished eating and poured some water into a

215

pan to wash the soiled plates. Within a few minutes, she and William climbed onto the wagon seat, Andrew flicked the reins over the backs of the mules and they were riding along the path again.

The walls of the fort were tall, made of hickory, and the pointed ends of the logs looked impressive in the late afternoon sunlight. There were two tall guardhouses at each corner, and Sammie strained her neck to see the top. "Look, William, see the men?" The boy looked up. "There, see, walking on the ramparts?" He nodded his head.

Andrew pointed the mules to a cluster of Virginia pines near the gates. Their trunks were gnarled and the leaves wilted from the extreme heat, but they would keep the sun from bearing down on their heads. The wagon stopped, and he jumped down and tied the reins securely to the tree. "Stay here. I'll see if we can get in."

"Hallo, the fort!" he yelled. One of the sentries looked down.

"Who goes there?"

"I'm Andrew Prescott, wanting to trade at the fort."

"Wait, there." He yelled at someone on the other side and the fort gates slowly swung open.

Sammie could see him watching them. A couple of men stood with muskets at the ready. Andrew went to talk to them. The man on the high wall continued to watch Sammie and the boy. She huddled in her seat and put her arm around the boy for reassurance.

Once inside the gate, Sammie was surprised to hear a familiar voice calling her name.

"Samantha? That you and your boy?" An officer, his coat

dusty, and his belly pushing at his belt buckle, removed his cap. "I thought I might see you again, the company being sequestered here a while. I brought you a package of letters from back home."

"You are?" Andrew drew up short, turning to his wife, "You know this man?"

"He's my brother, Matthew. You must remember; he came to the house after Kendall's slaves ran away. They found nothing and left shortly after."

"Ah." Andrew frowned for a moment, then his expression cleared, and he held out his hand to the man. "Aye, I recall now. You were the inquisitive one, Lieutenant Watson, company K." He looked around at the clusters of soldiers lounging under a large pine tree. "Where's the good Captain Blanchard?"

"He's gone on patrol. I'm the commanding officer today. Come to my office, and I'll give you a drink. You must be parched from traveling." He started to move away, but Sammie stopped him.

"Matthew, I'm pleased to see you again. I've purchases to make. Perhaps I'll see you before we leave, and I can get the letters from you then. William, come with me." Sammie walked away, her son at her side, glad to leave the men to themselves. Matthew was a stranger to her. She was still a little miffed that he had been so impolite when they last met. Her memories of Virginia belonged to another person. Kentucky was now her home, and the pampered life of that distant land was a dream she dared not entertain too many minutes at a time.

She returned to the wagon, her arms full of brown paper wrapped packages. A gangly youth of maybe twelve years followed with a box of food staples. The mules were grazing on the small pile of hay that someone had pitched on the ground for them.

"Thank you, Parsons, if you would just put the box in the wagon, please." She started unloading her arms of her burden, tossing the bundles into the wagon. William stood watching the boy, a look of admiration on his face. Sammie opened her cotton coin bag, took out a penny and gave it to the youth. He thrust it into his pocket.

"Ma'am, the lieutenant said I was to help you with whatever you needed done. He said you're his sister from Virginia, and I wasn't to leave your side for a moment." He took his cap from his head and raised his arm to run the sleeve of his shirt across his brow to wipe the sweat from it.

"But, I'm sure you would rather be watching the horse racing down by the river. Go on, I'll be fine on my own." She smiled at him. They could hear the cheers and laughter from the other side of the stockade.

The boy looked askance at her and grinned. "But, the lieutenant might tan my hide if I don't obey him. He's going to be my new papa."

"What? My brother's getting married? He didn't tell me. Where's your mother?"

He turned and pointed at one of the identical shelters under the low hanging roof covering the boardwalk around the perimeter of the stockade. "Over there, ma'am. That's where we live, my ma and me."

"I see, and what's your mother's name?" William was pulling on her hand and she looked down at him.

"Her name's Susie. Susie Parsons. I think the boy needs to pee, ma'am. I'll take him to the outhouse, if you'd kindly wait, and I'll take you to my mama. She'll want to meet the lieutenant's sister, I'm sure."

"Very well, thank you. I'll wait under the trees." She moved to the shade of the pine trees and watched as the two boys walked toward the shed near the general store, from which she had just come. She began to understand why the boy had been waiting for her to finish her shopping. She'd been surprised when he offered to carry her box. The merchant had called him Parsons, and she'd assumed that was his name; and he hadn't contradicted her. So, she thought, Matthew was getting married, and to a widow with a son. She frowned. But she must be much older than him to have a son as old as this one. Out of the corner of her eye, she saw Andrew walking towards her and turned to him when he moved under the tree.

"Hello, Sammie. Have you finished your shopping? Where's the boy?" She pointed to the outhouse and he frowned. "Alone?"

"No, there's a youth with him; a boy I met at the general store."

Andrew looked to the small room with the slanted brown roof. But, he didn't question her further.

"I was talking to your brother, and he's invited us to dine with him and his fellow soldiers tonight. I accepted on your behalf. I know you'll want to renew your acquaintance. I've made arrangements for you to spend the afternoon with a widow, Susie Parsons. Matthew recommended her. Said she's got room for you in her small cabin."

"Oh, Andrew. She and Matthew are to be wed. The boy told me. She's his mother, a Susie Parsons, he said."

"Married? But, he said nothing to me about it. Here they

219

come." And, they watched as William walked beside the youth, his hand firmly clasped in the large one. When he saw Sammie, he broke away and ran to her.

"Mama, Piney has a dog."

"A dog? Well, why don't we go and see this dog. Would you like that?"

"Yes'm."

The group moved to the cabin that Piney Parsons had pointed out earlier. He skipped ahead and ran in the door, shouting to his mother. She appeared at the door, her blonde hair tied in a red kerchief and her blue dress partially covered with a gray apron. Sammie could see that her eyes were blue, and she looked to be over thirty years old, by the wrinkles and dry skin. There was a small scar above her left eyebrow; very unusual, Sammie thought.

"Oh, my. You must be Matthew's sister." She brushed a strand of hair from her brow. "He said you were here. I'm so glad to meet you. Come in. The place is small, but I prepared some bread and potatoes and beans for your meal. I'm Susie Parsons, and this is my boy, Percival, but we call him Piney. Dear, fetch me some more wood, please."

"How do you do? I'm pleased to meet you. I'm Samantha. This is my husband, Andrew Prescott, and my son, William. Are you sure we're not causing you trouble? We've brought some food with us; but if we could have some water; that would be fine."

"No trouble at all. Matthew's told me about his large family in Virginia. Come in."

Susie Parsons led them into a small room, with a fireplace burning brightly and a table set with wooden trenchers as well as two battered pewter plates and pewter utensils. It had a gay red and white checked cloth on it and some wax flowers that looked slightly melted. Sammie could smell the aroma of fresh bread. There was only one chair, but a bench graced one side of the table. In the corner was a bed festooned with a multicolored quilt. On the opposite wall was a half-log shelf with a couple of lanterns and a framed portrait of a man in an Army officer's uniform. Andrew moved to the shelf and gazed at the picture.

"That's my late husband, Captain Homer Parsons; he was killed last winter by the Indians." She touched the surface of the painting with a gentle finger and sighed.

"The boy said you and Matthew are being married soon." Sammie started taking off her gloves and bonnet. It was extremely hot inside the small room, and she was perspiring profusely. Andrew walked back outside; she knew he was uncomfortable with female talk. William went out, and Sammie heard a dog barking.

"That's Sarge, our dog. I can't really afford a dog, but the soldiers help us feed him. He's popular with the men. They all regard him as their own. Sergeant Whitaker found him as a pup wandering around the fort. No one knows where he came from; maybe strayed from a settler's wagon. That's why we call him Sarge, after Whitaker." As she was talking, Susie was putting the finishing touches on her dinner. The room wasn't large enough for two women at the fireplace, so Sammie sat politely and watched.

Once, Susie went to the door and looked out on the parade ground at some soldiers marching to and fro, but she didn't say anything, just returned to the fireplace.

All seemed silent outside, and Sammie wondered where

William and Andrew had gone. As she was thinking of looking for them, Andrew, Piney and William came in the door. The room seemed even smaller with the additional people.

"That's a fine dog, Piney," Andrew said. William ran to Sammie, and she took him into her lap. "I saw Matthew coming from the headquarters cabin. He looks to be headed this way."

They filled their trenchers, as well as the two pewter plates, with food and moved out onto the grass to eat where it was cooler. Sammie gracefully accepted one of the trenchers, no longer minding the old wooden-style plates, since at home she could use her china anytime she wished. Matthew had brought a bundle of letters tied in a thin cord for Sammie. "Letters from home," he said. Her fingers itched to read them, but she would wait until they reached a place where she could enjoy in private.

As the afternoon drifted past, Andrew wandered off to water the mules and take care of his business, Matthew returned to his duties as temporary commanding officer, and Piney entertained William with the dog and his pony, while the women talked and knitted. Susie told her something of her background. She was born in Connecticut, but her parents had left their farm for Virginia and she'd met her husband there. He was a young officer at the time and worked his way up the ranks to the position of captain in the late war. As his widow, Susie was awarded some land, but she had no way of claiming it.

*****

The room in the officers' quarters was not much larger than Susie's home, and it was full of people as the sun lowered in the sky and a cool breeze blew through the treetops. The women brought hams, chickens, puddings and vegetables. It was spread on a plank held up by three barrels. As temporary commanding officer, Matthew had the place of honor, with Susie Parsons at his side. She wasn't only his betrothed, but the widow of a man of higher rank, thus, given the position at the head of the table. Sammie, Andrew, William and Piney sat along the side, with Sergeant Whitaker on their flank. Two of the local farmers were seated on the opposite side, with the blacksmith, Morstrem, and his wife, Lucy; the chaplain; and the proprietor of the store, James Flanagan, and his wife, Mattie, making up the rest of the party.

To the happy surprise of Sammie and Andrew, the celebration of Independence was to be also the day of Matthew's wedding. Immediately after the food was consumed, and with the remains still on the table, they took their places in front of the fireplace, and the chaplain read the words of grace over them. They said their vows with solemnity and reverence. One of the men must have been listening at the door, for a great burst of applause and cheering was heard outside, and the celebration really began, with fireworks and music.

Sammie sat with mixed emotions; she hadn't expected to attend a wedding while visiting the fort, and the groom was her older brother. She gazed at Andrew, and he had a queer look in his eyes. She turned away as a large burley man picked up his violin and began to play a lively tune. The merchant's wife sang with a clear bell-like voice a popular Irish ballad, and the dancing began. Sammie's heart was beating rapidly, but she was doomed to disappointment as Andrew whispered in her ear that he was going to the wagon. Since the newly married couple would be using Susie's room, they, Piney and William would be sleeping in their tent under the stars. They left the fort gates and made their way to the wagon. The moon seemed extra bright to light their way, and the sound of frivolity followed them long into the night. The air was stuffy inside the tent, and Sammie heard the sound of a dog wailing, but she soon drifted to sleep.

*****

The early mist hung in the treetops, as Sammie stirred the beans in her pot. She drew her cloak about her to ward off some of the chill. The gray smoke from her fire swirled upward in the slight breeze as she glanced up to see Andrew coming toward her with a rush basket in his hand. He stopped and grinned; Sammie heard sounds of whimpering from the basket and, startled, drew back as Andrew laid the basket on the ground and took out a small black puppy from the basket.

"Oh, Andrew." She squealed with delight as he placed the pup in her arms.

"I thought you might like some company, while I'm working in the field." He stood back and watched as the dog squirmed and whined in her arms.

"Oh, thank you, husband. What's his name?"

"He doesn't have one yet. I got him from one of the settlers whose bitch had pups on the road." He grinned. "You'll have trouble later on when he's grown. He's going to be a large dog; you can tell by the paws."

Sammie's attention was so concentrated on the puppy's antics, that she didn't notice the look of delight in Andrew's eyes as he turned away, seemingly embarrassed by his deed.

"I'll build a small house and pen for him, but you'll have to feed him. I'll tell the hired hand to help you."

She was awakened several times in the night by the whining and crying of the puppy, and finally took him into the pallet beside her. He felt warm, and she cuddled him until he fell asleep. Andrew pretended to be asleep, but she knew he was as restless as she and the dog.

Early the next morning, they left the fort and drove the distance to Cooper's Ridge, where Andrew bartered with the rest of the supplies he had brought. They didn't stay long as the colonel's plantation would need his attention. He couldn't leave the neighbor alone to care for his stock longer than necessary.

July 4, 1798

It has been a year since my last entry, & I've come to the last pages in my Journal. It's been a great adventure, coming into the wilds of Kantuckie. The new hired hand brought from the fort seems friendly enough. He lives at the Col's cabin, & I seldom see him. Hammond Jett is his name & he's a former Soldier, now retired. Our days are endless; A. works the land; the vineyards are drooping & won't make wine again this year. The tobacco, wheat & oats have been harvested & taken to Cooper's Ridge for selling. We've had a severe Drought so he has had to haul water from the creek in Barrels to wet the fields. The corn is Scorched & he was able to save a few acres. I've lost two chickens to the heat; but the rest seem to be well enough. Much excitement was had, as we traveled to Cooper's Ridge for supplies. It has grown to one Hundred settlers strong. My brother Matt. was married at the fort to a charming widow named Susie Parsons, who has a son called Piney. I pray they are happy in their new Life. As soon as his term of duty to the Country is over they plan to move to Lexington. The men celebrated Independence with horse & dog races. There was a band & Fireworks on the green. I was able to shop in the bakery & buy some pastries I had never tasted before. They are folded over with brown sugar glaze drizzled on top; delicious & a real Treat. My memory wanders to my mother's iced Cakes of long ago. A. bartered with two pigs for some bolts of cloth and shoes for William.

*****

Life at the farm seemed tame after the excitement of American Independence and the wedding celebration, except for one small event. The puppy, adventurous as all new life must be, constantly found new things to pique his interest. One of those was the chicken pen. The first few days, he delighted in running alongside, stirring them to feathered flight. Sammie enjoyed the sight, but she cautioned Andrew there might be trouble with the hens laying, if he continued. On the third evening, the birds began squawking fearfully. Rushing outdoors, they found the puppy inside the pen. He'd dug a hole under the fence and was having the time of his life playing with his new friends. Several of the chickens had managed to fly over the fence, and Andrew and Sammie spent the rest of the evening returning them to their enclosure. Andrew was angry at first, but when the small dog nipped at his feet playfully, barking excitedly, he couldn't help but laugh.

"This was my fault. I see that now." He lifted the puppy to look him in the face, but the animal squirmed until he was finally set free and ran off to bark at a passing butterfly.

"Your fault?" Sammie, tired as she was, smiled. "You helped him dig the hole?"

"You warned me, and I failed to see how the antics of one small dog could wreak such havoc. I've learned my lesson."

The next day, Andrew rode toward the forest, and soon, with the help of the horse's strength, pulled a large log to the wagon, stripped some bark from the branches and chopped away the twigs. Sammie heard him whistling. She was surprised for it was so uncommon a sound.

The next evening, as he had promised, there was a small crude shelter for the puppy and a fenced area for him to roam around in, while she did her chores. She tried to ignore his lonely cries as he grew accustomed to his new ownership. She called him Brutus, but Andrew called him Trouble, and she could see he had a certain gleam in his eyes when he said it. She laughed with him, as the dog began to follow her around, getting under foot, as she moved about the place.

Sammie tended the animals and her household chores. There were more chickens hatched, and a colt was born in the shed. William loved watching it frolicking in the field. She promised that as soon as it was bigger, she would teach him how to ride. The days lingered long, hot and dry. Andrew and the new hired hand worked the fields and chopped a seemingly endless supply of firewood for the winter. Sammie glanced out the door one early morning and saw a road gang come to fill the holes and clear the brush from the pathway. They piled the brush in the middle of the roadway and set it afire. Sammie took William up before her on the saddle and rode Dinah along the path for a mile to watch the excitement, the puppy scampering along beside her. There were maybe twenty men scattered along the passage, and they gawked at her as she passed. She returned to the house and cooked a chicken and dumpling stew with carrots and onions, along with a pot of turnips and peas for their dinner. On the third day, they had worked their way past the farm, and Sammie missed watching them work.

October 22, 1798

> *I have used most of the pages, & must conserve. I carried a pitcher of water to the hands Commissioned by the county to work on the Road, while the hams & bacon were smoking over the corncob fire in the yard. It has become quite a thoroughfare & is often used by Teams of horses & wagons carrying all manner of trading goods. A. and H. Jett were busy bringing in the hay harvest for the cattle. The weather has grown cold & wet & he anticipates a Hard winter. We saw two of Kendall's people walking down the newly widened road, following the wagons past the workers to the auction sale set for next Thursday. Kendall's men harvested his crops early this year, A. said. He suspects our neighbor wished to beat us to Market, but A. says our Tobacco is of a better grade, & he has already received an advance on the crops. I dared not Wave or speak to the dark-skinned men as strong feelings have*

arisen with the Advent of the settlers. The rough-hewed road workers jeered & scoffed at the black men. I left the Pitcher behind & went into the house; for a woman isn't safe when the Anger & resentment are aroused by the evil Practice. A. scolded me for my foolishness. The sky is darkening & I must put my Pen aside for lack of space. I see a few early stars, come out to Greet me & witness my Adieu from you, my little friend. Tomorrow, I will start a new book purchased at the fort.

— 20 —

In the spring of their seventh year on the land, Andrew received a letter from a lawyer in Washington, along with a large packet enclosed in pigskin and addressed to him. The letter said that Colonel Livingston had died in January, two months before, and was buried with military honors. The packet revealed a copy of his will and the deed to any property, either in Kentucky, Washington or Baltimore, made out to one Thomas Tully, Junior. He sat stunned as he read it through, and read it again. Andrew laughed until Sammie was afraid he'd be ill. He jumped onto the back of his horse without a saddle and rode across the property until the horse was breathing hard and wet with sweat. He dismounted and walked the horse to cool him and rode him home.

Sammie was sitting near the fireplace mending a tear in William's shirt. She looked up when Andrew came in the door. His face was pale, and his shoulders slumped. He put the musket in its place and turned to the fire.

She laid her sewing aside and said, "What's troubling you, husband? What has happened?"

He turned his head and lifted one hand to the mantle, leaning into the warmth of the flames. He sighed and began to explain, "The colonel has died and left the property to someone else."

Sammie gasped and held her hand to her mouth. Andrew withdrew from the fireplace and paced the room, his steps revealing his sorrow.

"I don't understand. How could he do this to you? You've filed the papers in the courthouse and sent copies to him in Washington."

"He had the option to change his mind, or give the property to someone else. There was nothing to stop him from withdrawing his support." Andrew clinched his hand into a fist and slowly released it.

"It's sixteen months after the five years of his claim would be legal and the military warrant proved. Surely, if someone else were coming to claim it, they would have done so already."

"Even so, I have no rights to the land." He knelt, somehow calmer, and worked at the fire with a slender stick that was charred at one end. "All my work, wasted."

"You'll feel better with something to eat. I have some hoecakes I can warm in a skillet. And meat to go with it."

"My stomach is distraught. Food won't stay down." He pulled up a stool and faced the fire, refusing Sammie's additional entreaties, and only once rousing himself to pat the dog on the head when he tried to get his attention. Eventually, he rose without a word and went outside into the dark of the evening.

That night he sat for a long time under the big oak that he'd left standing near the barn. Sammie worried about him. It wasn't like him to sit without moving for such a long time. She left the lamp burning and undressed for bed. The next morning, he was working in the tobacco fields again when she awoke. She drank a cup of coffee and pondered the years since her hastily arranged marriage. If Colonel Livingston had a hold on Andrew, he was free from the obligation now. Would it change him? If her mother knew how her marriage had turned out, would she be sad? Would she blame her father or herself for it? Sammie was tired; she felt so old and lonely and exhausted. She longed for the sight of her family; for someone who loved her. She cherished the time spent with William who was now running about the house and yard with ease and joyful laughter, playing with Brutus. He was such a happy child and gave her much pleasure.

She washed and put the cup away, then stood for a long time gazing at her husband working in the fields. He had such strength of character, even as he worked in homespun clothes and scuffed boots. She knew that he'd been forced to marry her; it was obvious he hadn't grown to love her, but she loved him. She longed for a word of kindness or a smile of joy when he came into the house. He'd grown into a solitary, hardened man. Would it always be this way? She could visualize the future ahead, lonely, bitter years. She cried for the lost opportunities, for the pain, the anxiety, the loneliness of Kentucky.

*****

A few months later, as Sammie was working at her quilting

frame, the dog began to bark, and when she quieted him, she heard the sound of a team and wagon. She set out the ingredients for bread, so the hired hand, if he saw her, would think she was planning to bake. She ran to the door and saw a whole train of wagons, not just one. The dog snarled at the throng intruding into his domain, and Sammie hushed him, holding him back from running after them. Oh, the thrill she felt as she watched them leave the roadway and file into the yard until it was filled with wagons, animals and people. At least a dozen women slowly climbed down from the wagons. Joy filled her heart, where only moments before, there was bitterness and pain. Andrew came from the field, leaving the surprised hired hand gazing after him, and talked with a couple of the men. He looked to the cabin and saw her standing with the women. He moved slowly toward her, accompanied by two men, one husky, with facial hair, and a long black queue tied with a black ribbon, broad shoulders and a barrel chest; the other slender, with a more refined look, his clothing of the finest society could buy, his hat sitting far back on his short brown curls. There was a faint familiarity about him, and a wave of premonition crossed her heart.

"Samantha, this is Thomas Tully. He's come from Baltimore to claim his inheritance of one thousand acres from the colonel. Will you bid him welcome? Sir, my wife Samantha, and my son, William."

Sammie was stunned. She could see the resemblance to a man she had seen visit her father many times when she was a child. She didn't know the younger man, but she knew the elder by reputation. It was rumored that he had killed a man during the late war, but his relations had appealed to the general, and he hadn't been indicted. This was the man who had inherited Colonel Livingston's land?

"Good day, Mr. Tully. Would you like a cup of tea? Or, perhaps you prefer coffee, instead?" She spoke politely, but William became fretful, and she picked him up for a cuddle. They entered the house, and Sammie put the boy in his crib and took her china tea pot and cups from the shelf. They were the only signs of her past as a wealthy merchant's daughter, other than her flowered plates. All else had long since been bartered for necessary supplies. She sighed as she reached for the tea tin.

"No, thank you, Mrs. Prescott. I cannot abide tea since the late war with England." He sat with his pearl-handled cane across his lap; his boots were shined and had a yellow tassel on the top cuff. His long trousers looked to be made of fine wool by an expert tailor. The dog hunkered in the corner, growling, but when Tully didn't come closer, he laid down his head and watched the man carefully.

"What? But, surely you're too young to remember the Revolution?" She looked to Andrew for confirmation, and he nodded.

"That's true, but my mother has described the terrible days to me. I sat for hours on end listening to my father and his friends talking of the taxes and the embargo of the ships in Baltimore Harbor."

Sammie could tell that he was prepared for a long speech on politics, and she listened politely while making a pot of coffee. She brought out some ham, boiled some potatoes and served the beans. Andrew inquired of their guest, "Mr. Tulley, it's been some months since we learned of the colonel's passing. If you wished to make a claim on his land . . ." He left his sentence incomplete. He watched the man, waiting for him to answer.

"Ah." Tully coughed and placed his napkin beside his plate. Sammie's treasured flowered china sat before him, his food partially consumed. The man's face reddened, as if caught in a moment of shallowness. "You see, there was the colonel's funeral to plan and certain legal matters to resolve. I was forced to liquidate some of my new assets." He attempted a smile, as if he didn't want to speak of it more. "Ah, plans had to be made to come into the Interior. They took longer than I had expected."

Andrew smiled politely. "Now, here you are for the rest of your inheritance. I see." The meal continued, with strained moments of extended silence, and finished, the men took their conversation outside. Sammie was relieved, for she didn't think Andrew was pleased to see his adversary come for a visit. She could tell he clearly wasn't comfortable in his presence.

This was borne out, as she cleaned the dishes, when she heard the jeers and taunts of men engaged in a bout of fisticuffs. She was shocked to peek through a crack in the door to see her husband and the colonel's heir pounding on each other with anger and hatred on their faces. She quickly glanced behind her to see that William was asleep and turned to find Andrew on the ground, blood coming from his nose. She gasped with shock and brought her hand to her chest to ease the pressure building in her heart.

Her pulse skipped a beat, but he rose and threw a heavy punch into his opponent's mid-section; and Tully curled up into a ball and lay in the dirt, winded. The dog burst through, barking wildly at the fallen man, until Andrew shooed him away. The watching men became silent as they witnessed their fallen champion. His hair was dirty, his fine trousers had a tear and his face was contorted in rage as he slowly rose to his feet.

"You'll pay for this, Andrew Prescott! I swear you will!" Sammie closed the door and went back to cleaning the dishes, frightened of the future. Her stomach roiled at the violence she had witnessed, and tears fell from her eyes. She used her apron to wipe them away.

At last, between the babble and exclaiming and scolding and cursing, the story was complete. They had come to build a town on Colonel Livingston's property. One of the men, a Thaddeus Blessingame, an experienced contractor and carpenter, had the plans from a reputable architect in Washington, with the town lots laid out in sections with streets and drawings for a school, a church, a courthouse and a town hall for community meetings. Samantha was shocked, and her pleasure at the arrival of the pioneer caravan turned to bitterness.

Andrew asked questions of Blessingame and showed him the proof of his ownership from the contract signed by the colonel, since he'd been the one who had built the house and the barn, and planted and harvested the crops as the colonel had sent him to do. With the organization required of a large party, the settlers soon set up their tents and campfires, and the women began cooking meals for their families. Sammie watched in fascination from her front door. As nightfall set in, she closed the door and sat in their one good chair as she pondered this strange happening. She was still there when Andrew came in and gently closed the door to keep out the insects.

He walked to the mantle and hung his musket on its pegs. He took off his hat, and boots.

"It was all for nothing, Sammie, my dear. I told them it's been nearly two years since the contract was fulfilled, but no one would listen. All our toil under the sun and rain and snow and heat. All for nothing." He bowed his head into his arms and wept. She rose and gathered him into her arms while his shoulders shook with his grief.

"I don't understand, Andrew, what's gone wrong? You've done what the colonel contracted with your uncle and you to do, selling the wheat, corn and wine, and sending him the profits. Why's that man here?"

He sat up and straightened his shoulders, and dried his eyes on her apron. He looked at her with such a penetrating glance that she thought he could see through to her bones. He rose and went to the small trunk in which he kept his private things. She'd never attempted to look at them, knowing that it would displease him. Slowly, he opened the metal box and brought out the papers, one at a time. There were the contracts between her father, Franklin Prescott and Colonel Livingston. There was the copy of their marriage license. And, there, still in the pigskin bag in which he received it, was the bribe. In stumbling, halting sentences and scrambled details was the evidence that she had suspected but didn't want to believe. He'd been paid in cash and promised the land, if he would marry her and bring her to this strange place in the wilderness. She sat stunned and knew that it was true.

"But, what has happened? You've done as the men wanted. You've completed the work on the land to fulfill the requirements of the claim and sent the profits back east as he required. Why does he now take it all away from you?"

He cautiously took one of the papers from the pile, and with a finger to point out the damning words, he showed her the secret clause.

"Read here. I'd hoped to never show you this. When news came of my Uncle Livingston's death, I'd hoped it could be forgotten." Andrew drew in a deep breath, as his face reddened in shame.

"Nothing can be so bad as you describe." Yet, as she took the paper, Sammie felt a shiver run down her body. She began to read the hateful words written in ink on the parchment from so long ago. The government contract hadn't given Andrew possession of the land, but the colonel. The contract with the colonel had promised the land to Andrew in exchange for the profits from the property, only restrained by a confusing morality clause.

"But, what have you done? I don't understand." Sammie brushed at her face.

"There was nothing I could do. I was forced to sign the clause, but that was foolishness on my part, I know now. I've been a fool. I hoped when I saw the news of Livingston's will, that no one knew my shame, only to be thwarted in even that."

"You've done nothing immoral. You've been a gentleman, and you've worked as hard as anyone I know." Sammie's hand shook as she lifted her face to gaze into Andrew's eyes, and tears began to run down her cheeks.

"I'm sorry, so very sorry." Andrew's voice broke. He explained that he could be rejected if any evidence emerged of any past indignities or behavior unbecoming a gentleman. It seemed it was the loophole that had stolen the land from them.

"Still, Andrew, I don't understand. Father told me that Colonel Livingston won the bounty lottery and was willing to finance your trip to the western wilderness, if only you had a wife to help with your endeavor. Why would my parents agree to this?" She thrust the paper in his face. She wanted to pull her hand away, but he held it fast.

"The colonel expected greater profits than the land provided. He promised to invest some of it in a home that would someday be yours." He stopped, his eyes red. "I was desperate for the land. Your mother didn't want the marriage to go forward without assurances you would be provided for, but your father persuaded her to continue." He dropped her hand and walked away. A look of rage and anguish crossed his countenance, and Sammie felt compassion for him.

"There's more, Andrew. I know there is. Why would the colonel change his will?" Without looking at her, he cleared his throat, and she could see his shoulders droop.

"I had gained a certain reputation. When I was in Kentucky the first time, I lived with an Indian woman. She had a child, a boy." He turned to Sammie. "The boy still lives. Somewhere in this vast wilderness, I knew a child of my loins lived. My uncle Prescott knew about him, but not Livingston. I've now learned from Tully that his father told the colonel, and he was very angry, thinking I had deceived him about my past. He would have denied me the chance to live in this place I'd grown to love, if he'd known. I signed the contract, and he found the action contemptible. Can you understand, Sammie?" There were tears in his eyes, and he bowed his head in shame.

"A boy? You have a bastard son, a child of Indian blood? When the Indians attacked Hicks and Gerrard, you knew the men, didn't you? You had lived with them, ate their food and hunted with them. You mated with one of their women. Wait!

The child at the fort?"

Andrew reeled in shock. His face turned parchment white. "You saw them?"

"Was that your woman? Your child?"

"No. No, please, Sammie. I knew them, yes; the child's father was a friend. He was killed in a raid on some settlers and I grieve for him. The woman has married again. They are going further west, away from the encroaching civilization. I was glad to have a chance to say farewell." He gave a sigh of regret as he looked away from her.

"Why didn't you tell me?"

"I didn't know you, my dear. You were a stranger. That first day in your father's house, when I gazed into your face, I knew I'd made a mistake. You were so young, so innocent, so charming and brave. I wanted you. I'd never been thwarted in my physical desires before. It was devastating to think that I would be denied your body, your lovely charms. So, I continued with the charade. When confronted with the truth, I signed my name to the morality clause, knowing it was a lie. Please forgive me, Samantha."

"What's to be done now?" The words were so faint as to nearly not be said at all.

"Tully inherits all, the thousand acres, the property in Baltimore and in Washington. All is lost to me."

Sammie Prescott, for all her strength of character and of body, simply fell onto the floor in a dead faint. It was too much for her tender heart to endure. All was in vain. Andrew picked her up gently and took her to the bed and laid her there. He went for some water and a clean cloth. He bathed her forehead and she came out of her swoon, but she wouldn't look at him. He rose and left her.

*****

He couldn't go outside, for there were the settlers to witness his shame. They wouldn't know the truth, of course. He had made sure of that with his beating of Tully and had his promise. But, he didn't trust the man. He was human and an animal, just as those in his barnyard. He put another piece of kindling on the fire and made a pot of coffee; not because he wanted coffee, but for something to do with his hands. He heard a faint noise and looked up. Sammie stood in the doorway, her face pale; her eyes looked sunken in their sockets, and he felt a knot in his throat. Nausea threatened to engulf him.

"Andrew, you've lost the inheritance of the colonel, but there's our own land. It's only three hundred twenty acres, but it's been yours free and clear for two years. Hasn't it? You've built a cabin and the outbuildings, and planted and harvested crops for seven years. Isn't it yours? Oh, dearest man, please say that this house and land are yours."

Andrew looked at his wife, stunned. She was right. He'd worked the land and built the cabin, while also working the Livingston land. It was rightfully his; there was no secret obligation to his family. He had made careful calculations, walked off the boundaries, with Josiah Ferguson, Jess Bond, Frank Gentry and Sanford Kendal as witnesses. Not an inch of this land was on the Livingston claim. He watched as she turned away, and suddenly as though a bright light shone on the horizon, he realized the truth. He loved Samantha. It had been growing slowly through the years, and he hadn't recognized what he now saw as the truth. But, would she believe him now? Would she think he simply wanted the land, not her? He crossed to the child asleep in the bed, and his love almost overwhelmed him. He'd denied it; had mocked it and almost hated this small person who had come between him and his desire for property and the acclaim of society. He reached out one shaking finger and, for the first time, he touched the living example of his virility; a son of his own flesh and blood; whom he could openly claim as his own. His heart seemed to pound at an alarming speed.

He pulled the hot coffee pot off the spit and sat down, his head in his arms. He had to think; to work out in his mind what to do. After a long time, he raised his head. He knew what he must do to win her respect and love. Nothing else seemed important to him now. He kindled the fire, checked that everything was well, and blew out the lamp. He crept into the bedroom so he wouldn't awaken her if she was asleep. He removed his clothes and slowly eased his way onto the bed.

*****

Sammie wasn't asleep. She had listened to the movements in the kitchen and ached for his arms around her; even if he couldn't love her, she loved him with her whole heart. If it was possible, she wanted to take away his disappointment and pain. She heard him come into the bedroom and held her breath. She heard the rustle of his clothing as he removed them. Her heart raced with joy. He was coming to her tonight. She barely breathed, she was so pleased. When he moved onto the bed, she scooted to his side. She was afraid he would reject her, but he didn't. She felt daring; she felt her heart swell to the highest mountain as he accepted her offering of her body to solace his mind. He placed the tiniest of butterfly kisses on her mouth; and she opened her lips and tasted the sweetness of hope. He kissed her again, harder, and she opened her heart and arms to him. For the first time since their marriage, he was gentle and kind, and she rejoiced in the feel of his arms and body. She fell asleep in his arms.

*****

Sammie felt wonderful. She opened her eyes and blinked, for he was still with her. He hadn't left her alone in the bed. She reached out her hand and lifted the tuft of hair from his forehead that always fell when he didn't comb it down. His eyes opened, and she held her breath, afraid that he would reject her. He smiled, and she smiled back. He didn't move, just lay there smiling.

"You are so beautiful, Samantha. I love your smile and your sweet touch on my body. Please don't leave me. Don't ever leave me, my dear, for I think I would die if you weren't here to give me your warmth and advice and generous self. I love you. Do you understand, sweetheart? You've given me hope when I thought all was lost. We'll start anew. You were right. This property is small, but it's our home. Will you stay with me, Samantha, and be my wife forever? Will you teach me to love our son and care for him?"

"Really? You really love me? You aren't afraid of my love?"

Andrew rose in the bed, his naked torso pale in the early

morning light from the window. He drew her into his arms and she rested with her head on his shoulder. "I think I must have fallen in love with you the first time I saw you, but there was the obligation to the colonel, and to my uncle and your father. I was a fool. I can see it so clearly now, when it was darkness before last night. It took the entrance of the settlers onto our farm to make me wake up from the nightmare. No, don't break away, for I cannot say what I must if you look at me." He held her gently in his arms.

"I was always ambitious, I think, and had visions of roaming the mountains and trapping beavers since my earliest days. To be free and unfettered; to hunt and fish and sleep when I wanted. I thought of having my own place; thousands of acres of wilderness where I could wander freely and no one to tell me to leave or push me off my land. I came to Kentucky the first time with a group of hunters and trappers, and I fell in love with it. The wide roiling streams, the wild animals, the cane breaks, the open meadows; it was all a dream. I worked for several years as overseer on a large plantation and hated the restrictions on my time and freedom; I hated having to follow the orders of my employer who abused his workers, even me. It was several years before I had a chance to come again to Kentucky. By that time, I had gained more wisdom and experience. When my uncle learned of my dreams to live in Kentucky, he searched for someone who needed an experienced backwoodsman, and discussed it with his brother-in-law, Colonel Livingston. He'd been awarded the military warrant for his services in the war, but was too old and infirm to come and settle here. It was a mutual need, I guess. He needed someone like me; I needed a patron, someone to finance my venture. It was when they suggested that I have a wife that I began to object to the plan. I didn't want to marry; even less to have children." He paused, whispering, "I know what I'm saying must hurt your gentle heart. You grew up in a large family and naturally expected children of your own to love and cherish. Please don't be offended, Sammie.

"Colonel Livingston was eccentric in many ways. He never married himself, but he believed in marriage. He had no children, but he loved children and worshipped his neighbor's children. Jemima is his sister, and he loved her only child, Nate. He insisted that the settlers would come more enthusiastically to the area if I was married. I resisted. My uncle used his influence, and finally, I was called to the colonel's home and told that he had found a bride for me, and if I wanted the money and the parcel of land, I must marry her. That was you, my dear, Samantha. Somehow, your father was let into the deal, I don't know exactly how. He wrote his acceptance of the marriage offer, but they insisted I make Nate my heir if I perished in the wilderness. It fit right into my plans."

He was silent for some time, and Sammie was growing anxious. She could hear the settlers at their campfires and thought that she should probably get out of bed and take care of her child and the animals. Surely, they wouldn't steal her animals, would they? She moved out of his arms.

"I need to get up and see about the animals. The settlers might decide to steal them." She laughed bitterly, but she could tell that Andrew hadn't thought of the possibility. They began to get dressed.

"This conversation isn't over. We'll talk later." The papers from his metal box were still on the table, and he took the ones he needed outside.

She went to the fireplace, built up the fire and started to cook a meal. William was aroused and dressed. He sat and ate his porridge, while her heart ached, for she had so longed for children of her own. She was dismayed her husband didn't want children. Andrew? How did he feel toward William? What had he felt when the child was born? Had he resented him and his presence in their home? Oh, how he must have hated her. He had proclaimed that he loved her and asked that she teach him to love the child.

The matter was yet unresolved, but she knew this one thing. She wanted him. If he would stay with her on their cozy farm, then she would accept his decision and shower him with all the love that was rejected during the lonely years. She went to the door and saw that several of the men were saddling their horses. Andrew was talking to Blessingame. He had the papers in his hand, and she knew that he was explaining that this property on which they were camped was not on Livingston land. Blessingame spoke to the men, and the people began to board the wagons and drive away. Andrew stood under the oak tree and watched them go.

And, suddenly, as though a dam had broken, the water came flooding from her eyes. But, they were tears of joy and gladness. She picked up her child and swung him around the room. He laughed, and she laughed with him. "He loves me, William, your papa loves me. He said it, and I believe him. We have no large property, only this small plot of ground on which we stand, but we have you, and I am so happy."

— Epilogue —

It took years before the land in dispute was finally settled. A surveyor was brought in. Jess Bond, Sanford Kendall and several of the original settlers swore in depositions that the land boundaries had been clearly marked when they arrived, and the Prescott farm was not included in the vast Livingston military warrant. Other settlers swore in court that Andrew had worked the Livingston property and his own claim alike during the required five years, and the original owner, Colonel Obediah Livingston, had never stepped foot on the land, and it should have rightfully been awarded to Andrew Prescott.

By the time the courts agreed on the settlements, it wasn't nearly as important as had been originally thought, for the ones who had laid claim to Andrew's farm had given up their case and moved further west. The town was built, including the school, the church, the community center and a fire station, as well as a hospital, a bakery, library and livery stable. Thomas Tully returned to Baltimore. Matthew was retired from the

Army and living in Lexington; Charlotte and her family lived in Illinois; Thomas was married; and Marguerite also. Young John Watson was sent to military school, for his father had political ambitions for his youngest child. Letters now regularly flowed back and forth between the family members with the mail service. Jemima Crockett was alive and well, but Franklin Prescott was dead and buried, when Andrew Prescott, proudly holding his son by the hand, and his wife, Samantha, descended the Federal Courthouse steps in Lexington, their claim permanently settled by the law.

The year was 1803, and Thomas Jefferson was president of the United States. A widower, he and his daughter, Martha, replaced the Adams family in the large gray sandstone house on the Potomac River; and the city boasted of 6,000 citizens. Under his administration, the commissioners reached an agreement with Napoleon to purchase the Louisiana territory for about 15 million dollars, and America was on the way to expansion to the Pacific Ocean.

Samantha had no more children, and she grieved secretly for them; but with such a large family, there were nieces and nephews aplenty to come for a visit, and she cherished the time spent with them. Eventually, Andrew cleared all his land except for the oaks, hickories, willows and evergreens that he left standing as shade for the animals. He didn't resent the loss of the larger property and silently watched as it was divided into smaller and smaller sections, until the free open wilderness that he loved was no more. He was content with what he had wisely set aside for himself. It was a small farm, but it met the needs of the couple who lived there until their deaths.

The property was left to William, sole heir and child of

Andrew and Samantha Prescott. At the age of five and twenty years, he met and fell instantly in love with their neighbor, Miranda Patterson. When they married, the properties were combined; and in a strange twist of fate, both houses, and the vineyard planted by Andrew Prescott and Josiah Ferguson, belonged to the son and grandchildren of Samantha and Andrew. What a surprise that would have been had Colonel Livingston lived to see it.

www.ingramcontent.com/pod-product-compliance
Lightning Source LLC
Chambersburg PA
CBHW071302250626
47159CB00004B/1270